BEFORE
I GO

BEFORE
I GO

BRIAN
CHARLES

JOHN SCOGNAMIGLIO BOOKS
KENSINGTON BOOKS
www.kensingtonbooks.com

JOHN SCOGNAMIGLIO BOOKS are published by

Kensington Publishing Corp.
119 West 40th Street
New York, NY 10018

All Kensington titles, imprints, and distributed lines are available at special quantity discounts for bulk purchases for sales promotion, premiums, fund-raising, and educational or institutional use.

Special book excerpts or customized printings can also be created to fit specific needs. For details, write or phone the office of the Kensington Sales Manager: Kensington Publishing Corp., 119 West 40th Street, New York, NY 10018. Attn. Sales Department. Phone: 1-800-221-2647.

The JS and John Scognamiglio Books logo is a trademark of Kensington Publishing Corp.

ISBN: 978-1-4967-3639-0

ISBN: 978-1-4967-3640-6 (ebook)

First Kensington Trade Paperback Edition: October 2022

10 9 8 7 6 5 4 3 2 1

Printed in the United States of America

To Abby Marie and Nolan Matthew

PART I

LOSING HIM

SPRING

Chapter 1

Landing

Monday, May 16
10:22 p.m.

It's easier to die when you don't see it coming. The stealth approach of a heart attack or the sudden strike of a car accident offers no opportunity to dwell on what's to come. Neither allows time to contemplate life—the loved ones left behind and the dreams left unfulfilled. But when an airplane falls from the sky, slowly gliding toward the cold, black ocean, there's nothing subtle about death's approach. It's coming. It's inevitable. And, in Ben Gamble's case, its slow advance left too much time to think. The gap between knowing his flight was fatal, and actually crashing, allowed time for worry and doubt. Time for panic and anxiety. And far too many minutes to contemplate regret.

The letter shook in his hands as turbulence rocked the cabin. Ben tried to read it again, but a sudden dip in altitude forced his eyes closed. He was a coward for keeping the secret from his wife. Now that the chance to tell her was gone, it tortured him to imagine her finding out from someone else. He opened his eyes and looked out the plane's window into the night. He wondered what his secret would do to her. He wanted the chance to explain. Wanted one last opportunity to talk with his wife. Taking his gaze from the window, he read the last line of the letter again.

You need to tell your wife, Ben. She deserves to know the truth. I'll give you this week. Otherwise, I promise to tell her myself.

Ben folded the letter and shoved it in his pocket. He looked back to the window and the inky black night beyond. But soon something formed in his vision. It took a moment to understand what he was seeing—the moon's reflection as it glistened on the surface of the ocean. It came closer and closer until the water reached up and grabbed the airplane. The impact was jarring. Held in place by the seatbelt around his waist, his body lurched forward. He crushed his nose on the headrest in front of him, felt the blood cover his upper lip and drip down his chin. Screams erupted through the cabin, and his vision blurred as his seat vibrated. After the initial shock, though, the plane skidded along the surface for several seconds, the water rushing by as if Ben were on a speedboat.

Enough time passed as they glided along the ocean's surface for Ben to believe the pilot had miraculously pulled off the emergency landing. But when the right wing dipped into the water, the plane somersaulted violently. The contents of the cabin—from luggage to food, soda cans to passengers—rattled around the inside of the aircraft like a shaken snow globe. Ben's body lurched to the side and he cracked his head against the window. The impact sent a spider web through the Plexiglas. His world came to a standstill as he watched the cracks spread, a circle of impact centered within the twisting fissures. The nucleus of that shattered window held many images as he stared at it. Everyone in his life peered through that hole at him. He saw his mother and father. His siblings. He saw friends and colleagues and the partners from his firm. Finally, when the screaming disappeared and the whining engines quieted, when the shrieking metal finished tearing apart and the cold Pacific Ocean crept over his skin, he saw his wife. Her beautiful face and radiant smile made him want to stick his finger through that hole in the Plexiglas, then his hand and his arm and his whole body until he could climb from the sinking tomb to hold his wife and protect her from his secret.

When the icy water crept over his face, it jolted him into action. He reached for the buckle on his seatbelt and unclipped it.

Chapter 2

The Call

Tuesday, May 17
4:00 a.m.

Abby Gamble's eyes fluttered as she slept. A moan escaped her lips while she was deep into her dream. She and Ben were headed off on vacation and, as was typical, running late. She hurried behind him as they raced through the airport's parking lot, her rolling luggage tipping as she ran. Each time she righted herself, Ben was farther ahead. When Abby made it to the escalator, Ben was already at the top of the stairs and heading for the tram. She took the stairs two at a time, her suitcase banging along behind her. When she made it to the platform, Ben was waving for her to hurry through the still-open tram doors. Abby tried to run, but her luggage became lodged in the top of the escalator, like the loose shoelace her mother had always warned would be sucked up by the revolving stairs.

"I need you," she heard Ben say.

Abby looked up. The tram doors were closing.

"I need you with me!" Ben said again, just as the doors closed.

She gave up on her luggage, dropping the bag to the ground, and ran toward the train as it began moving. Slowly at first, almost inviting her to jump on the rail and take an easy ride to the terminal, then picking up speed and blurring past her until it was out of sight. When she looked back to the escalator, the steps continued to revolve until they ingested her suitcase.

Abby's eyes opened and she bolted up in bed. She briefly felt for Ben next to her before gaining her bearings and remembering that he'd left on a business trip. A surge of adrenaline filled her system. The alarm clock told her it was just past four in the morning. She climbed from bed and went to the kitchen for a glass of water, recalling her lethargic jog through the airport parking lot during her dream. Just once she wanted to be a sprinter in her dreams, free from the heavy-legged running she always experienced and able to bolt from one place to another. Abby sipped water and listened to the quiet house. The hallway clock ticked, and the air conditioner hummed.

I need you with me.

She checked the clock again and knew he wouldn't mind if she woke him. Ben never minded late-night calls when he was away on business. She dialed his number, but his phone went straight to voicemail, which meant he'd either turned it off or run the battery down to nothing—both unlikely. Something had her out of sorts, so Abby paged through the folder in the kitchen until she found Ben's itinerary. She scanned the information and came to the number for his hotel before it occurred to her that his flight hadn't even landed yet. She closed the folder and took a deep breath. No wonder his cell went straight to voicemail—he was thirty thousand feet over the Pacific Ocean.

Her shoulders were just starting to relax when her phone rang. The sudden chime in the quiet house startled her. She slowly moved her gaze to the microwave clock again as her phone continued to ring.

I need you with me.

She slowly picked up her phone. The caller ID registered as *Transcontinental Airlines*. She let the phone ring a moment longer before swiping the bar and pressing it to her ear. She allowed a long second to pass before she spoke.

"Ben?"

"Hello, Mrs. Gamble?"

"Yes?"

"This is David Peirce from Transcontinental Airlines. I'm afraid there's been an accident."

Chapter 3

The Families

Tuesday, May 17
6:57 a.m.

At just before seven in the morning, the Chicago headquarter offices of Transcontinental Airlines were immaculate, quiet, and ominous. A TransCon representative met Abby in the lobby and took her hand as if she were a dear relative at a funeral.

"Mrs. Gamble, right this way," he said.

"Have they located the plane?" Abby asked as the man led her to a row of elevators.

"It's a developing situation. We'll have more information after we get upstairs."

They rode to the thirtieth floor and the man led Abby into a glass-walled conference room where a few other worried family members were already waiting. They all glanced at each other, wanting, but not daring, to ask if this were really happening.

Airline employees with troubled expressions served coffee and donuts. Within ten minutes, thirty-some people filled the room. Eventually, a distinctive looking man, dressed impeccably in a suit and tie, strode through the doorway and took his spot at the front of the room. It was easy to tell this man was in charge. All eyes were immediately on him as everyone waited for good news. Bad news. *Any* news.

"Good morning," the man said. "My name is Paul Bradford. I'm the executive vice president of TransCon here in the Midwest. Let me start by first expressing my regret over this unfortunate situation. Our thoughts and prayers are with your loved ones. Let me get right to the details."

Bradford clicked a remote, which brought a ceiling-mounted projector to life. A satellite image of North America appeared on the screen behind him, and a curved red line demarcated a flight path from O'Hare International Airport to Los Angeles.

"TransCon flight 1641 originated from Chicago, took off on time and landed at LAX at seven p.m. last evening. The plane was refueled, and a routine maintenance check cleared the aircraft for the trip to Sydney, Australia."

Bradford clicked the remote and a world map popped onto the screen. Another red line materialized, this time originating in Los Angeles and moving in the same arched manner toward Australia. But halfway across the Pacific Ocean, the line stopped.

"Five hours and twelve minutes into the flight, Transcontinental Airlines 1641 experienced an explosion in the forward cargo bay."

Gasps filled the room, then crying. Paul Bradford offered a brief pause before continuing.

"The explosion caused the engines to ingest fuselage debris and both engines were lost."

More gasps and murmurs came from the family members.

"What do you mean the engines were *lost?*" someone asked.

"The engines ingested debris from the explosion and were no longer functional," Bradford said.

"But isn't there some sort of safety power supply?" the same man asked.

"Yes, the APU—the auxiliary power unit. However, from the data our engineers and analysts have gathered, we suspect the APU failed."

"Your *analysts?*" the man asked, anger in his voice. "Forget the analysts. What are the pilots telling you?"

Bradford took a deep breath. "The pilots were able to confirm that both engines were lost. But shortly after that transmission, the aircraft suffered a total electrical failure and we lost all communication. That's why we suspect the APU also failed. A functioning APU would have allowed us to continue receiving and transmitting to the aircraft."

"So what happened to the plane?" a woman in the back asked.

"The explosion occurred at an altitude of thirty-four thousand feet. Without communication, we can only speculate about the course of action the pilots took. Standard protocol, however, when faced with engine and APU failure, is to rely on the ram air turbine. The RAT generates power from the plane's air speed and is able to provide hydraulic capabilities that allow the pilots to steer and glide the aircraft. It's our belief that, using the ram air turbine, the pilots attempted an emergency water landing."

Another chorus of gasps came from the family members. Abby placed her hand over her mouth, remembering her dream from just a few hours before—running after Ben, trying to keep up. The tram doors coming together and closing while his words hung in the air of the empty platform.

I need you with me.

"NTSB has been working the situation from the very beginning of this crisis."

Bradford turned back to the projector screen and circled an area in the South Pacific with his laser pointer.

"Based on the plane's location during our last communication with it, we have extrapolated the area where the pilots might have ditched—" He cleared his throat. "Where the pilots likely attempted the emergency water landing."

He clicked the remote and several lines appeared connecting the West Coast of the United States to Australia.

"These are shipping channels and are filled with cargo boats twenty-four hours a day. The NTSB has alerted the captains of cargo ships in the area we believe the landing may have taken place. Those shippers are essentially the first responders, and we're hoping to hear good news from one of the boats in the area. We have also been in contact with the US Navy, and ships are en route to the area now."

"The engine failure happened five hours after takeoff," another family member said. "That was midnight. It's now seven in the morning. Why haven't you found the plane? Or life rafts? Or anything?"

Bradford cleared his throat. "The Pacific is still currently under the cover of darkness. But we hope as day breaks that we'll have a visual and more information."

Silence followed as everyone in the room stared at Paul Bradford, wordlessly begging for information he did not have. Aching for confirmation that their loved ones were safe. Abby stood from the conference table and steadied herself with a hand on the rich mahogany before walking slowly out of the room, a noticeable quiver to her gait. The starched-suited vice president of Transcontinental Airlines offered no more details about the location of the plane. He didn't have to. Everyone in the room knew why the plane hadn't been found. It was a giant piece of metal that flew into the ocean and sank like an anvil.

Chapter 4

A Watch and a Wallet

Friday, May 27
10:15 a.m.

The doorbell rang, and she considered ignoring it. This was Day Ten, a week and a half since Ben's plane had disappeared, and there was still no trace of it. Cable news ran constant coverage of the missing Transcontinental plane and the two hundred forty-seven passengers it held. Abby turned the television off after Day Four and hadn't turned it back on since. The doorbell rang again. She pulled herself from the kitchen chair and walked to the foyer. When she opened the door, a man stood on her porch in a stiff suit and blinding white shirt. Over the past ten days, Abby had grown tired of starched suits and shiny ties. She wanted an airline representative to show up in faded jeans and a T-shirt to break the bits of bad news they came to deliver. Wearing a suit somehow made it worse.

"Mrs. Gamble?" the man asked.

Abby nodded.

"I'm James Darrow with Transcontinental Airlines."

"Come on in."

Along with his somber face, James carried a leather folder. Abby led him to the kitchen where they both sat at the table, across from each other.

"Can I get you something to drink?"

"No thank you, ma'am."

Abby pointed at the folder "What's the latest?"

James Darrow ran his hand over the leather dossier and took a second before answering, Abby assumed, to gather his thoughts.

"A small debris field has been located. We've confirmed that it came from Flight 1641."

Abby sat up straight. This was *real* news, not the redundant garbage they had fed her over the last few days.

James placed the dossier onto the kitchen table and opened it. He pulled a graph paper grid from inside, unfolded it, and slid it to the middle of the table so they both could see.

"This is a grid of the search area," James said.

Abby had seen this graphic before, nearly every day for the past week and a half, and still the vastness of the ocean took her breath away. On the grid was a red oval that represented the presumed area where Flight 1641 had gone down. The red oval was situated inside a larger elliptical, this one demarcated in yellow, which represented a more expansive diameter of the search area. And finally, a green rectangle outlined the whole thing, denoting the area that experts felt represented the farthest possible path the plane could have traveled after both engines failed. Coordinates of latitude and longitude marked each location.

"Here," James said, pointing at the page. His finger touched the edge of the outer green rectangle. "NTSB located a pair of cabin seats as well as some pieces of luggage."

Abby licked her lips. "Were they floating?"

"Yes, ma'am."

"Why is it so far away from the red circle?"

"Well," James said, "we're not certain, but we have some educated guesses. The explosion happened in the forward cargo bay, so we believed the contents of that cargo bay were scattered in an area of the ocean quite a distance from where the aircraft actually touched down. Based on the discovery of this debris field, our engineers and analysts are rethinking the flight path and designing new models that will redefine the search area."

Abby waited. She knew there was more.

"I know you've heard the math before, Mrs. Gamble, but the search area is vast. The engine failure happened at thirty-four thousand feet. If the aircraft was powered only by the ram air turbine, which we believe to be the case, then it averaged two thousand feet of altitude loss per minute. That means it glided for roughly fifteen minutes and covered over one hundred miles before it touched down. The calculations on all that produce an area of over thirty-two thousand square miles that needs to be searched."

Abby sniffed and wiped her nose, determined not to cry. She had grown hysterical during a few of these meetings, mostly in the initial couple of days, as information first leaked to the families. She remembered little of what had been discussed during those meetings and forced herself to keep it together now, willing herself to concentrate until James Darrow from Transcontinental Airlines had delivered all his information.

"Life vests were still secured to the bottom of the seats that were recovered," he said. "So we fear that there was never an opportunity to deploy them."

She took a deep breath before she spoke. "Which row were these seats from?"

"Twenty-four."

"But Ben was in first class," Abby said softly, her lower lip trembling.

"Yes, ma'am. Mr. Gamble was in row four. But in this area," James again pointed to the grid. "Luggage was also discovered. Mrs. Gamble, some of the luggage pieces belonged to your husband."

Abby looked up from the grid to find James Darrow staring at her. Her vision blurred.

"No," she said, shaking her head. "You said these seats were from coach. From the back of the plane."

"Yes, ma'am. But luggage has been discovered from throughout the aircraft. In one of the suitcases, personal items were recovered."

James reached into the inner breast pocket of his coat and pulled out a plastic bag. Abby shook her head when she saw it, the tears welling on her eyelids for only a second before spilling down her cheeks.

"I need to ask if you recognize these items, Mrs. Gamble."

He placed the plastic bag on the table. Abby reached for it. Still shaking her head, she opened the bag and with trembling fingers pulled out Ben's watch. She recognized it immediately—it had been her birthday gift to him. Still, she turned it over to be sure. The letters *BDG* were engraved in cursive on the backside. Benjamin Dempsey Gamble. The plastic bag also contained his wallet, which she retrieved and paged through. His driver's license was front and center, and Abby cried full out when she saw his picture—giant sobs that she was helpless to control.

"I'm sorry," James Darrow from Transcontinental Airlines said. "Can I call someone for you?"

Abby shook her head as she continued examining the contents of Ben's wallet, still wet with salt water. She vaguely heard the starched-suited man tell her that the search-and-rescue effort was being downgraded to a recovery-only mission. She comprehended very little. All she could do was stare at the photo of her husband and wonder how it was all happening again.

THE HOLIDAYS

Chapter 5

The First Thanksgiving

Thursday, November 24
1:32 p.m.

In the six months that had passed since losing Ben, Abby Gamble found little joy. The pain came in waves, sometimes lapping at her feet, other times crashing down from overhead. But no matter the intensity, it was always there. Constant and incessant. Sleep was a torment because it was there that she found him. It was in her dreams that she felt his touch and knew his scent; heard his voice, even. She lost herself in those dreams and in her memories of him. The dreams were so lucid that she came to accept them, believing every time that they were reality. Trusting that Ben was there in front of her. That his embrace was sincere and his kiss authentic. Some part of her subconscious was always leery at the start of those dreams, but eventually she gave in to the temptation. Just as she relinquished her doubts and succumbed to her desires, submerging herself in the belief that he was back in her life, she would wake. There was always a moment of struggle, just after opening her eyes, when Abby fought against reality and worked to convince herself that this time would be different. That she would explore the emptiness of the bed next to her and find him buried beneath the covers, the warmth of his body like a fire to curl up next to. But those seconds were fleeting, and eventually her fingers clawed but could not keep hold of the fantasy. It was then that she would become fully alert and painfully aware of her husband's absence. The nightly ritual was like losing him all over again, and sleep eventually became something to avoid.

Abby had taken a month to herself after she lost him. It was a month of seclusion and isolation that consisted of no work and little human interaction. Her sister, Maggie, had been her only conduit to the outside world. But after that first month, Abby slowly filtered herself back into the life that waited. Work became her refuge. Twelve hours a day, during which she avoided troubling thoughts of how she would cope without him. Her career represented a great source of pride, and she had poured much of her life into her business. It was an easy crutch. A twelve-hour break from the suffering, a painkiller she prescribed daily—as addictive as any narcotic. She knew the addiction well. She had fallen under its spell once before, many years ago, when her life had been rattled and derailed much like it was now.

For the past six months Abby had felt the concern of those around her and put up a façade to appease them all. Once or twice she had made it to dinner with Maggie and friends. She trekked to her parents' house each Sunday to show them she was healing, although she felt a loss in her soul she was sure would never mend. Losing Ben had produced a second crater in her heart that neighbored the first. But that original asteroid had struck many moons ago and, although still deep and devastating, the scar from its impact had healed over. To the point, at least, where she could explore its topography and come out unscathed.

It hadn't always been that way. When the damage was first done—when she and Ben lost their son, Jacob—she ran from the pain and used the analgesic of her work for as long as its potency lasted. When it wore off, though, Abby was forced to assess the damage. Only then, and with the help of the man she loved, had she been able to recover and put her life back together. Jacob's death changed the life Abby had once known, made it different and unrecognizable. But when she made it through the pain and anger, she found that as long as that life included Ben, it was one she could continue living.

But now he was gone. Who would help her navigate this time through the caverns and crevasses of her loss? She was alone, left by herself to collect her bearings and find her way. And Abby knew the hardest time was coming. Winter was approaching, which meant Christmas was out there some-where. She never really considered it possible to spend the holidays without Ben. But here she was, standing on her parents' front stoop on Thanksgiving Day without him.

"Hi, sweetie," her father said when he answered the door.

Abby pushed a smile onto her face. "Happy Thanksgiving, Dad."

She handed over a bottle of wine and a pumpkin pie.

"Hey, sis," Abby said when she walked inside.

"We could've picked you up," Maggie said.

Abby shook her head. "I'm not sure how long I'm staying. Not feeling a hundred percent. I've got a little stomach thing going on."

It was her go-to excuse of late. A way of cutting an outing short when she needed an exit strategy. Or, sometimes, avoiding them altogether. But Thanksgiving could not be skipped, Abby knew. So here she was.

Maggie took Abby's hand. "You're not going anywhere. Mom needs help with the stuffing."

The football game was playing in the background and

Maggie's husband was sitting on the couch with his feet on the coffee table.

"Hey, Abby."

"Hi, Jim."

"Don't get up," Maggie said. "God forbid you miss a second of the game."

Jim lifted his beer and pointed at the screen. "The Bears are about to . . . it's tied and . . ."

But the women were gone before he could finish.

"Happy Thanksgiving, Mom," Abby said when she walked into the kitchen.

"Abby! Where have you been? You were supposed to come early and help with the stuffing."

Abby gave her mom a hug.

"I got held up waiting for the pumpkin pie to come out of the oven. It's still hot. But I'm here now, so put me to work."

The three Hartland women fell into their usual routine, moving around the kitchen, adding salt and cinnamon to the stuffing, checking the turkey, and whipping up the gravy. For Abby, the smells and the sounds and the voices all brought back childhood memories. But every time she glanced into the family room and saw her father and Jim watching football, the scents and sounds faded away and all she noticed was the one thing that was missing.

An hour later, when her family sat around the dinner table holding hands and saying prayers of thanks, she knew they all secretly wondered the same thing: How could Abby Gamble be thankful? First Jacob, and now Ben. It was happening all over again.

Later on Thanksgiving night Abby sat alone in her house. In four weeks Christmas would arrive, but Abby knew there would be no tree this year. No stockings or decorations, either. Nothing, in fact, that might bring Ben's image back to her. The man loved Christmas in a magical way that always reminded Abby of her childhood, and embracing the holiday without him would feel like she was letting him go. It would feel like she was moving on and forgetting about him, and Abby was a long way from being able to handle those emotions.

It was cruel, Abby thought, how memories of such wonderful times could be so sharp as to cut, so painful now that instead of welcoming them she worked to avoid them. Erase them until a different time, in the future maybe, when the edges had dulled and they were less dangerous. She curled into the couch on that Thanksgiving night with a glass of wine and a trashy paperback, uninspired by the words but still looking to them to aid her escape.

Chapter 6

Sisters

Thursday, December 15
12:06 p.m.

The snow fell like feathers that refused the pull of gravity, adopting instead their own schedule and flight. It dusted the shoulders and caps of the Christmas shoppers who walked Michigan Avenue, their feet crunching over the accumulation on the sidewalk. Abby sat with her sister at a window table of the Grand Lux Café and watched the activity below. Hundreds of people, wrapped in scarves and parkas, carried bags and packages to their next destination. It was Saturday afternoon, two weeks before Christmas. A hectic time for most, as deadlines approached and time collapsed, but a strange calm had come over Abby. She had already completed her shopping. Her list was shorter this year; for better or worse, she simply had fewer people in her life. The past six months had spawned no new relationships, and many old ones had died with her husband. Friends had dropped out of sight; some not close enough to lend a supportive voice, others nervous to stir up unwanted memories. Ben's friends, whose wives Abby had socialized with, were there for her initially, but their presence faded with time. Her close friends were present with phone calls and texts, but none had pushed too hard to pull her back into their social circles, worried, Abby was sure, that the act of them living their normal lives would spin Abby further into despair. She wasn't sure if they were correct, but in the end Abby was just as guilty. She hadn't tried too hard to find her way back to them. But eventually she would. She'd pick up the phone someday and call her friends. Abby would filter back into their lives, and they into hers. It was another part of the process she would one day go through. At this point, though, her wounds were still wide and gaping. Not yet sutured together and certainly in no condition for others to see.

It was more than friends who had fallen out of Abby's life. Ben's mother had called that first month or two after the search was called off, but there was something in Janet Gamble's voice that offered too strong a dose of her son. They met for lunch just before Thanksgiving, and Abby knew it was something she would not soon repeat. In her mother-in-law's eyes she saw her husband, felt him in her embrace, and heard him in her voice. Abby knew Ben's mother was having the same problem talking with her son's widow. So they sat, two women whose lives had been shattered, each unable to help the other sort the pieces. They left the restaurant that day promising to do it again, assuring each other they would keep in touch, but knowing it was a lie. Neither could be part of the other's life until they each had driven through the smoky haze of pain and torment Ben's death had left behind. So two weeks ahead of Christmas, Abby Gamble's circle had tightened to her sister and her parents. Shopping took no time at all, and she found herself wanting to fast-forward through the season.

"Next Saturday," Maggie said, sitting across from her, "Jim and I are going to this dinner party. Why don't you come along?"

Abby pulled her gaze from the activity on Michigan Avenue, smiled at her sister, and took a sip of cappuccino. Maggie Hartland was a duplicate of her sister. Four years younger than Abby and still the two were mistaken for twins.

"That would be perfect," Abby said, gently placing her mug down. "A dinner party filled with couples, and I'd show up by myself. No thanks."

"Actually . . ." Maggie said, averting her eyes from her sister's the way she normally did when trying to back Abby into a corner. She looked out the window and casually glanced down at the pedestrians walking the street, as if her next comment meant nothing. "There'll be a lot of single people there. And there's one guy in particular that I want you to meet."

Abby raised her hand. "No thanks. Definitely not."

"Come on, Abby." Maggie regained eye contact. "It'll be fun. You need to get out of that house and away from your office."

"And go to a dinner party with a bunch of people I don't know? I can think of nothing worse, Maggie."

"You'll know Jim and me."

"No thanks. I'd rather go stag to a wedding and sit for dinner with a bunch of strangers."

"Okay, we'll skip the dinner and the four of us will go out."

"The *four* of us?"

"Yeah. I want you to meet Mark. He's great."

"Maggie!" Abby said with her head cocked to the side.

"Why don't you just meet him? He's nice looking and normal. I promise."

"Thanks, but I don't think so."

"It's just dinner, and we'll make it early so you can—"

"Margaret Marie Hartland," Abby said, locking eyes with her younger sister and using her calm voice, which was much more effective than yelling when it came to dealing with Maggie. "I'm. Not. Ready."

Maggie smiled awkwardly and then stared down at her cappuccino. She shrugged her shoulders. "Okay."

The rest of lunch played out silently, and the distance that had separated them for the last few months grew a bit wider. For two women who had always been able to share the most intimate parts of their lives, meaningless small talk was never part of their banter. It showed.

"It's really coming down out there," Abby finally said.

"Supposed to get five or six inches."

"Is that what they're calling for? Wow, it'll be a mess."

Maggie nodded, and they both stared out the window until the waitress mercifully brought the check. They joined the crowd on the Magnificent Mile, and Abby helped her sister pick out presents for the rest of the afternoon as they walked Michigan Avenue. They shared a cab home, and after her sister was gone Abby asked the driver to drop her in Lincoln Park, two blocks from her townhome. She needed to walk and clear her mind. And she needed the cold air to help. She pulled her scarf tight and sank her hands deep into her coat pockets as she made the turn east. Walking into the mouth of Lake Michigan, Abby felt its frozen breath, which was wicked and strong. A nasty gust momentarily held up her progress as she crunched over the compacted snow. She loved her sister, her parents too, but none of them knew what she was going through. Not now and not a decade earlier, when another devastation had rattled the foundation of her life and nearly brought it crumbling down in pieces.

Abby crossed Lake Shore Drive and found an empty bench that offered a view of the lake. Belmont Harbor was a hundred yards to the north, empty and isolated—the sailboats had been stored for the winter, and only vacant slips remained. The temperature was in the teens, and the lake breeze dragged the wind chill below zero. But as Abby sat and stared into the vastness of the lake, the frigid temperature went unnoticed. Thoughts of her son anesthetized her body and numbed her skin. She closed her eyes and was twenty-five years old again.

The pain of her delivery was gone now, the epidural still lingering, and what remained was a heavy fatigue under which she was unable to crawl. The labor had lasted nine hours. The delivery was another ninety minutes of pushing and breathing that in the end was deemed uncomplicated. "Unremarkable," the doctor told them. Her baby, however, had been rushed from the room in a flurry of chaos, cradled by doctors and nurses who materialized from nowhere.

"When can we see Jacob?" she asked a nurse who came to check on her.

"They're running some tests. It'll be a couple of hours, sweetheart. Don't worry, this is very common." The nurse's voice was too pleasant. Too calming. Like a flight attendant cheerfully recommending that passengers cinch their seatbelts for upcoming turbulence. "Why don't you get some rest, and we'll wake you in a bit."

She stared at Ben, who rubbed her head and brushed a stray hair from her face. "She's right. Take a nap. I'll wake you as soon as he's back."

Abby bit her bottom lip. She had yet to hold her son. "Something's wrong, isn't it?"

Ben kissed her forehead. "Jacob's going to be fine."

So long ago and Abby could still remember those words as if they had just been spoken. And here she was, a decade removed from that day, reliving a strange parallel. But this time around, as she walked through the shattered remains of her life, Ben was not there to help her.

When the bite of the air became too much, Abby stood from the bench and turned her back to the lake and her thoughts. She walked two blocks to her townhouse, a slow stroll despite the sting on her cheeks.

In her bedroom she changed into a comfortable pair of sweats, running her hand over Ben's suits hanging in the closet—a neat row of tailored jackets that hadn't moved in six months. An errant tie had slipped off the rack and fallen to the floor. She replaced it, pulling the thin end until it balanced just perfectly to match the others. From the closet she walked to the dresser and picked up his wallet, which was resting in the same spot where Ben used to place it after work. Abby had set it there after James Darrow from Transcontinental Airlines returned it to her, as though Ben might come home and slip it into his pocket. His watch was there, too, and tears came to Abby's eyes when she placed it to her ear, listening to the second hand tick as if somehow she might feel her husband's presence come to her across time.

Chapter 7

A Backpack

Thursday, December 15
4:04 p.m.

Powerful winds whipped along the ocean's surface and churned the water while lightning ignited the sky in bright pulses cloaked by storm clouds. Massive waves rose out of the sea and reached up to the heavens, peaking in curled whitecaps that were twenty feet high. Rain poured down from above and blurred the distinction between ocean and air. Through it all, the backpack endured. It rode one colossal wave after another, disappearing in the roiling whitecaps high in the air before falling back to the ocean and sinking deep beneath the water's surface.

The journey continued through the night, a redundant sequence of the dark and angry ocean spitting the backpack out of each wave before swallowing it again. As morning broke, the sun rose from the horizon to penetrate the lingering storm clouds, coloring them a rich auburn. One final wave took hold of the backpack and launched it again. This time, instead of crashing back into the ocean, it landed on a beach. The wave crashed down onto land, and surf sprayed across the sand. The backpack somersaulted onto a web of crisscrossing bamboo that held onto the canvas as the wave retreated, back into the ocean. Three or four inches above the ground, the lattice of bamboo prevented other waves from recapturing the backpack. After a long and tumultuous journey, it had finally arrived.

The kid was walking on the beach when he witnessed the swell crash onto shore. He noticed the backpack tumble onto the bamboo. He lifted the soaking rucksack, unzipped the top, and peered inside. Finally, he shook the bag dry, hooked the strap over his shoulder, and continued his trek up the beach. After half a mile he turned inland and walked along the edge of the lagoon until he came to his cabin, where he gently deposited the backpack outside the door. Then he walked inside to check on his father.

He was not doing well since the plane crash.

Chapter 8

Christmas Eve

Saturday, December 24
1:22 p.m.

The phone calls had started early in the morning on Christmas Eve and were relentless. Abby knew their intentions were sincere, but on that day she needed to be alone. She'd put on her smile and get through the next day with her family. Currently, however, she was not able to conjure the will to fake it.

Maggie was with Jim and his family, and after her third invitation, Abby had to again showcase the calm voice to convince her younger sister that spending Christmas Eve with her brother-in-law's family was the last thing she wanted to do. Maggie finally conceded but promised to be over with cappuccinos first thing Christmas morning.

Abby's parents were another story. The calls started at eight that morning and had been incessant.

"The Coopers and the Sullivans are coming like always," her mother said. "Why don't you stop by for dinner?"

The Coopers and the Sullivans were parents of old grade-school friends, and Abby was sure that reminiscing about events from twenty years ago was not what she needed tonight—especially because talk of the past would eventually lead to talk of the present, about who is married and who is not, about who has kids and how old and what grade. Abby pictured the screeching halt the conversation would take when they all turned their attention to Abby. Awkward discussion of weather and work would follow. The thought made her cringe. Christmas Eve at her parents' simply wasn't going to happen.

"It'll just be the six of us," her mother continued. "And Bruce and Carol haven't seen you since—" Abby's mother cleared her throat. "Well, they haven't seen you for a while and I'm sure they'd love it if you dropped by."

Abby could extrapolate from her mother's sentence and was well aware of the last time she had seen Bruce and Carol Cooper. It was the last time she had seen many of her parents' friends, many of her own for that matter, and it was in August, three months after Ben's plane had gone down and soon after the search-and-rescue operation had been changed to recovery-only. The last time she'd seen her parents' friends was the day everyone gathered at the funeral home to kneel before an empty casket and say good-bye to her husband. Christmas Eve, with her emotions high and fragile, was not the right time for Abby's introduction back to the real world.

"No thanks, Mom. I'm fine."

"We have plenty of food. Maybe just for dessert, then? Just stop to say hi."

"Mom, I need to be by myself tonight. Really. I need this. But Maggie and Jim are picking me up tomorrow, and we'll be over by noon. Have fun tonight and *please* stop worrying about me."

There was a long pause. Then finally, "Okay, sweetheart. If you need anything, your father and I will be here. Just call."

"Thanks, Mom."

"And get ready for tomorrow; your father has been fermenting his glögg wine for three days. I'm almost used to the smell."

"Oh boy," Abby said with a chuckle. "I can't wait. See you tomorrow, Mom. Merry Christmas."

As she ended the call, Abby could almost smell her father's glögg wine. It was a tradition that ran back to her childhood, and something her father worked hard on each year—a giant vat steaming on the stove that held the awful concoction called glögg wine. It was no secret the wine was intolerable, but the effort put forth by her father—three days of mixing, tasting, and fine-tuning, and then all of Christmas Day brewing and simmering—was enough for everyone to manage a glass. The wine got worse each year, a strange anomaly of inverse proportion where more effort resulted in a lesser product, but her father always believed it to be a terrific creation. Ben had played into it each year and had always been convincing. She remembered Ben and her father in front of the fire and next to the tree, both taking hesitant sips before nodding and lying about what a grand creation it was.

Just as Abby was collecting herself with a series of deep breaths after she ended the call with her mother, the phone rang again. She answered, expecting her father this time, a final effort, but instead she heard another voice. Ben's mother.

The last time they had talked was on their lunch date a month earlier. As Christmas approached, Abby had thought many times about where she should spend Christmas Eve. She had spent the last twelve years at Ben's parents' house, and part of her felt she should be there now. But even over the phone her mother-in-law's voice brought to the surface those feelings of loss, the same as on their lunch date. Abby knew that Janet Gamble's house on Christmas Eve was an emotional breakdown waiting to happen. Attempting to recreate Christmas Eve without her husband was a surefire way to undo any healing Abby had managed over the last few months. Perhaps next year would be different, but Abby had resigned herself to the fact that she needed to spend this Christmas Eve alone.

"Merry Christmas, Abby," Ben's mother said.

"Thanks, Janet. Merry Christmas."

"Abby, I feel horrible I haven't called sooner. Of course, you know you're always welcome here. If you don't have plans, we'd love to have you for dinner. The regular crowd is coming, and it wouldn't be the same without you."

"Thanks, Janet. Gosh, I should have called you last week to let you know—I'm going to my parents' tonight." It was an easy lie.

"Oh, I feel terrible that I didn't reach out sooner."

"Don't. I told you I'd get a hold of you, and I dropped the ball on that. It's my fault. But I promise we'll have lunch again soon. We need to catch up." The lie was a little harder this time, but she managed without stumbling.

"I'd love that. Are you sure you're okay tonight?"

"I'm fine, Janet. Absolutely. Thanks so much for calling."

"Okay, sweetheart. If you need anything, just give us a call."

"I will, for sure."

"Merry Christmas."

"Merry Christmas to you."

Abby hung up the phone and decided not to answer it again. It never rang.

Chapter 9

The Journal

Saturday, December 24
3:22 p.m.

The coconut was buried in the sand, and from its core sprouted a bud that had grown to three feet in height. It produced a single, impressive frond. It wasn't much, but it would do. From the lone leaf he hung wild berries threaded together with fibers from a different coconut's husk. He rigged a small, fossilized starfish to the top of the shoot. When his creation was finished he stepped back to analyze his work. Considering the scarce resources of the island, it was an impressive-looking Christmas tree.

His neck itched and he ran his fingers through facial hair that had grown thick and long. He sat down in his chair outside the small shack he called home, lifted the journal from the backpack, and inspected it. The hardcover exterior was now soft with water damage, and the pages inside—bloated from having absorbed seawater—pushed the hardcover open like the petals of a blooming flower. He looked at the other shack that stood a short distance from his own and was grateful that William—the teenaged kid with whom he shared the island—had acted so quickly after he saw the back-pack wash up onto shore. Despite being waterproof, not even the backpack's Gore-Tex exterior could fully protect the journal after so long in the torrential ocean. Thankfully, the kid did the rest. William had spent two days salvaging the journal he found inside the pack, laying it in the sun and smoothing out the damaged pages. The tight binding that secured the cover had prevented the interior pages from succumbing fully to the ocean, and after two days under the hot sun the spine had dried, and the damp pages had recovered. The ink had held, and nearly every page was legible. The few sections that were unreadable were not lost, however. It didn't take much for the man to recreate those ruined passages. They remained sharp in his mind from when he had written them. It was a story he still knew by heart.

Opening the journal now, he thumbed through the passages and stopped at the heading:

The Day I Knew I Loved Her

He turned the page and read.

It was my secret spot. I went there to manage the pressures of college whenever clear-headed studying was necessary. Unlike the library or many of the campus education buildings, whose secret study nooks had long ago been mined and robbed of their worth, the third floor of the fitness center was a true sleeper and a gem of a discovery. The young architect inside of me analyzed the room when I first came upon it and immediately saw its potential. Dark and dreary, and packed with 1970-style exercise equipment covered in a thick layer of dust and time, I suspected I was the first person to enter the room in many years. This was a good thing. As was the steep and narrow staircase that led to the abandoned space on the third floor—it promised privacy.

When I noticed sunlight spilling through the half-moon window and streaking across a large oak table that rested in front of it, I knew I'd found the perfect study spot. It took a few days to spruce the place up, but by week's end I had the space looking decent. The dust and cobwebs disappeared. I stacked the exercise equipment on one side and covered it with a tarp. The heavy oak table was centered in front of the window, and I set a lamp on its surface to study by. As the semester progressed, the quiet nook on the upper level of the fitness center became my favorite place.

I had the privilege of owning a set of keys reserved for a select few students deemed responsible enough to open and close the fitness center. The third-floor attic, with its skinny staircase and dark stairwell, was a taboo location long forgotten. Years and graduations and turnover and retirement had erased from campus any students or faculty who ever knew this peculiar place existed. It had to have been years since the old exercise equipment had been dumped there. Until I stumbled onto it, the space was simply a neglected storage room on the top floor of a campus building. Now it was my hidden sanctuary.

I studied there often, usually after hours when the fitness center was empty and quiet. Occasionally I spent the better part of the night in my secret fortress cramming for exams, always sure to slip out before the center reopened in the morning. The place belonged to me and me alone. But that would change on a cold December night during my junior year. I locked myself in the secret nook for an all-nighter to prepare for my last exam before Christmas break. Then, at midnight, I heard it. The creaky wooden stairs whining under the weight of rising footsteps.

There had never been a visitor to my private sanctuary. To my knowledge, no one knew this space existed. My heart pounded as I sat in the darkened room. When I swiveled my chair toward the entrance, I saw her. The doorway framed her figure and the sight of her burned itself into my mind like the afterimage of a camera flash. The light from the stairwell fell across her features— shoulder length auburn hair and olive skin, a face that was immaculate and beautiful, ivory-white teeth that were perfect and straight when she smiled, which she did when she saw me.

"Oh, sorry," she said. She placed her hand over her chest. "Christ, you scared me. I didn't know anyone was up here. I'll let you study, sorry."

"No, no. There's plenty of room."

I'd have been an idiot to say anything else. I gestured at the empty spot across from me.

"Really," I said, trying not to sound like I was pleading. "There's room if you need a place to study."

"You sure?" she asked.

"It's the last night of finals week. There's no way I'd kick you out."

I moved my books to one side of the sturdy oak table. As she approached I extended my hand.

"I'm Ben."

"I'm Abby."

Our hands came together. There was something intoxicating about her smile, and there's no way for me to explain what it did to me that night. All I can say is that her smile never stopped affecting me the way it did that night. The wind whistled over the glass of the half-moon window and chilled it with an icy frost. We talked more than we studied that night, and when the sun peeked over the horizon just after six the next morning, we snuck down the creaking stairs and slipped out the back door.

Five years after that first meeting, young and athletic, Abby was hardly showing when the technician ran the ultrasound probe over her stomach. You were growing in her womb, and I knew my life would never be the same.

He looked up from the journal and reminisced about the time in his life when he wrote the passages. The journal contained a series of letters a grieving father wrote to his son after losing him. The letters had been therapeutic. They were a conduit to a different time and place, a way to break the boundary between life and death and communicate with the son he had lost. So it was natural, in these journal entries to his son, to start with the story of how he met Abby, and how he had fallen head-over-heels in love with her.

He directed his attention to the small coconut tree sprouting from the sand, with the tiny wild berries he had hung from its lone leaf and the starfish secured to the top. He replaced the journal in the backpack and stood from his chair. Walking into the forest, he unfolded a Swiss Army knife as he approached the tree at the edge of the foliage. The bark was missing in a jagged area near its base, exposing the smooth trunk underneath. He touched the tip of the knife's blade to the side of the tree and carved a vertical notch to match the others. They were arranged in groups of five—four vertical lines with a diagonal slash through them to create a collection of five days and make more manageable the task of calculating how long he had been on the island.

Ben Gamble counted them again, like he'd done a hundred times before. He ran through the calculations in his head. If he had it correct, it was Christmas Eve.

Chapter 10

The Cards

Saturday, December 24
5:13 p.m.

Abby spent the afternoon of Christmas Eve wrapping presents for her parents and Maggie. She set the presents in the corner where she and Ben usually placed the tree. As she backed away she imagined it, adorned with colored lights and saturated with ornaments. It was the first time all season she wished she had decorated.

Fueled by a surge of Christmas spirit she had worked all season to suppress, she padded down the basement stairs and headed to the corner. Boxes of Christmas decorations were stacked tall. Abby rummaged through them until she found what she needed, grabbed the box with both hands, and then headed back up the steps and into the kitchen. The box contained eight heavy porcelain mugs, the surface of each carved and molded into a white-bearded Santa Claus. Ben had given her the mugs for Christmas a few years back. He found them on a business trip in Hamburg, and they had appeared from the basement about the same time every year—at the frontier of the season, when the magic was just a faint tingle, like the first flakes of a coming snowstorm. The mugs had floated to her memory as she and Maggie browsed Crate & Barrel two weeks earlier, but Abby had decided to leave them dark and buried in the basement. Now, however, on Christmas Eve, she found the strength to retrieve them.

She filled a kettle with water and placed it on the stove, then climbed the stairs and headed for her bedroom closet. A few minutes later she carried an old department-store box down the stairs as the kettle whistled. In the giant Santa mug she poured a thick hot chocolate and topped it with whipped cream, which she powdered with nutmeg before cozying into the couch.

With the box on her lap, Abby removed the top and riffled through the contents. Inside were scores of letters and cards Ben had written her over the years. She had kept every one, dating back to the first Hallmark card he left for her, on the old oak table in their study fortress on the third floor of the fitness center where they first met. Over fifteen years the stack of letters had grown to quite a collection. Although she was not ready to face the world on Christmas Eve, it seemed fitting to spend the day that had been her husband's favorite reminiscing about their love story. It was something she could not have done a month ago. She had spent a great amount of energy over the last few months trying *not* to think of Ben. The pain was too much when she did. But tonight she needed him. Tonight she *felt* him.

Abby started with the Christmas cards and hung on every word. The early ones, written during their courtship, contained long columns of prose, and she studied them carefully, wringing from the page the memory of falling in love. It had happened only once in her lifetime.

At the bottom of each card, just before his name, was the closing Ben had placed on everything he had ever written her. A reminder that his heart belonged to her until the end of time.

I love you (forever)
        —Ben

Looking at Ben's signature jetted her off to their study fortress in college. It was the end of their junior year and after just a short few months, they both knew they'd spend their lives together.

"How about you?" Abby asked.

They were sitting at the oak table with the half-moon window next to them and a dark campus beyond. It was just past two in the morning and their cramming was winding down. The room was lighted only by the soft glow of the desk lamp.

"How about me? What exactly are you asking?" Ben said.

"How many girls have you been in love with?"

Ben closed his textbook. The table was covered with notebooks and papers. "You really want to get into this?"

"Absolutely."

"Nothing good will come from it."

"It's important that I know."

"Why is it important?"

"How many?" Abby asked.

"This is so stupid."

"How. Many?"

"Two, besides you. Both in high school."

"And?" Abby asked, waiting for his confession.

"And what?"

"These girls that you loved, did you also sleep with them?"

Ben creased his forehead. "Are we really going to do this?"

Abby stared at him with eyes like daggers. "Did you sleep with them?"

"No. We read poems together."

Abby sat upright. "Oh, you dog."

Ben laughed. "I dated each of them for over a year. And for what it's worth, I thought I loved them both."

"You thought you loved them?"

"Yeah, at the time."

Abby shook her head. "I've fallen in love with a dirty, filthy mutt of a dog."

"If I'm a dirty dog, what does that make you, Ms. Honda Civic?"

Abby had just made her own confession, of her first time. It was a convoluted story of a high school sweetheart who had not only briefly stolen her heart but also her virginity— in the back of her parents' Honda Civic.

"It makes me an innocent girl who had her heart broken."

Ben rolled his eyes. "Broken heart, maybe. Innocent, no way." He leaned closer to her. "Civics are so small you'd have to be an acrobat in order to . . ." He shook his head and leaned back. "See? Nothing good. Just like I told you. Now I'm mad."

Abby's eyes grew wide with seduction. She stood and moved closer to him, sitting on his lap and straddling him. With her eyes locked on his, she positioned herself, sliding her hips just right. "Don't be jealous, Ben Gamble." With her hands on his shoulders she leaned forward and kissed his lips.

He moved his hands to the silky slope of her thighs, his fingers creeping under the folded hem of her shorts.

"Uh, uh, uh," Abby said, pulling back and waving a correcting finger. "One more question."

Ben looked confused. "What is it?"

"If you only thought you loved those other girls, how can you be sure that you're in love with me? Maybe this is just a passing phase for you, like the others."

"No," Ben said. "I'm sure." He tried to kiss her again.

Abby pulled back. "How can you be so certain?"

"*Abby,*" *Ben said in a calm voice she would later learn to use with her sister,* "*It's two o'clock in the morning. I've got a final exam tomorrow. I'm slightly nauseous from listening to my girlfriend's rendition of how she lost her virginity. And now you're asking irrational questions about how much I love you. I don't know what's going to happen tomorrow with my exam. I'm not sure when the nausea will settle, and I know I'll never be able to ride in a Honda again without being* really *uncomfortable. But I know I love you. I'm sure of that.*"

She forced a smile. "*Still, though. I mean, summer's coming. Then our senior year. Then, who knows? We may not even be in the same city. How do I know—*"

"*Because I'll love you forever. It doesn't matter what year it is, or what city we're in.*" *He took her face in his hands.* "*It'll be forever, Abby. I'll never screw that up.*"

She read Ben's closing again as she stared at the card.

I love you (forever)

She read those words a hundred times on Christmas Eve. They appeared at the bottom of every note and every card. She read them while curled on the couch, the fire popping, her mug of hot chocolate keeping her company. She read them until she cried, and until her eyelids grew heavy with fatigue. She read them until she fell into a sound sleep, where she found her soul mate running through her dreams as if he were still alive.

PART II

NEW BEGINNINGS

THE FOLLOWING SPRING

Chapter 11

The River

Thursday, April 13
5:32 p.m.

The evening shadows lengthened as six o'clock approached. The Keaton boys figured they had just enough time to cross the river and circle home before dinner. They envisioned bolting from the forest at the back of the house and slipping through the screen door, past their father's den and into the kitchen where they would crash into their seats and wait for their father to emerge from upstairs and take his spot at the head of the table. Depending on the timing, they might whisper a few details about the adventure to their sister, making sure Brandon, their older brother, heard everything. They would never look at Brandon. In fact, they would pretend he wasn't there as they dished details to their little sister about how the river was up and how they had crossed anyway. How the two younger brothers had accomplished something Brandon could never do. Brandon had always been cautious, aborting each crossing attempt when the river was high and raging by telling his younger brothers that it was too dangerous.

If the two youngest Keaton boys could work it just right today, they'd mention to their little sister that it was their fourth time crossing the river this summer, that they didn't need Brandon to lead them any longer, and that maybe some-day they would invite Rachel to join them. They'd throw it all out just before their father sat down at the dinner table, so that Brandon would be unable to respond. Maybe they'd show off the dirt on their pants as proof. It would be an epic moment. An adolescent coup that marked a passing of the torch and a coming-of-age story for the two younger Keaton boys that meant they no longer needed their older brother to look out for them. But they needed to pull it off first.

The brothers came to a spot now where the river nar-rowed. A sturdy log stretched from the bank and wedged it-self between two boulders that poked up and broke the surface in the middle of the raging river. The fast-flowing water crashed around the rocks in a white fury, producing a growl loud enough to force the boys to yell when they spoke. On the far side of the river a fallen tree trunk butted against the rocks and would complete their journey across the water.

Log + Rocks + Trunk.

It looked like an easy formula and was definitely the best option they had come across after nearly a mile of walking the riverbank.

"Here. We'll cross here."

Joel Keaton, the youngest of the three Keaton boys, exam-ined the path that his brother pointed to. He noticed the gap between the rocks in the middle of the river and the fallen trunk on the far bank. "How do we get from the rocks to that tree trunk?"

Joel's brother noticed it now, the short distance between the structures. "We might have to jump. It'll be fine."

There might have been better options if they'd continued to search, but they needed to cross the river soon. Walking a mile back to the overpass and getting home, even if they cut through Gentry Cemetery, would put them on the other side of six o'clock. Explaining why they were late, with dirty pants and muddy shoes, would not be easy.

They looked once more upriver to the overpass in the distance. Two cars crisscrossed as they passed over the bridge in opposite directions. There was always the possibility that their father would be called into surgery. It happened once every week or two, and they ate dinner without him. Taking on their mother with muddy shoes and dirty pants would be an easier challenge, but they couldn't count on their father being late. They looked back to the river.

"We can make it," Joel's brother said. "It'll be fine. Let's go."

They each climbed onto the fallen log and stood up. With arms out like tightrope walkers, the middle Keaton boy led his younger brother along the thick and sturdy log that fed into the middle of the river.

Joel Keaton sat in an uncomfortable, vinyl-covered chair next to the hospital bed. His elbows rested on the armrests with his fingers interlaced and pressed against his forehead. A nurse walked into the room.

"Anything?" she asked.

Joel blinked at the sound of her voice, which pulled him back from his memories of the river. He looked up, saw the nurse, and shook his head.

"No. He's been pretty quiet."

The nurse adjusted the pillow as the man in the bed moaned. Joel put his hand on the man's shoulder.

"Take it easy, Dad. She's just trying to make you comfortable."

The nurse checked the IV drip, looked up at the wall clock. "He can have more morphine in an hour. I don't need to tell you, Dr. Keaton, but it's all about making him comfortable now."

Joel nodded, then leaned close to his father's ear. "Pain meds in an hour. Can you make it?"

Another moan. Joel looked up and thanked the nurse, who smiled sympathetically as she left the room.

Joel waited until his father settled down and the moaning stopped. Then he sat back in his chair and let his mind return to his childhood. To his brother, the raging river, and the terrible tragedy that had taken place nearly thirty years earlier.

Chapter 12

The Promise

Thursday, April 13
9:05 p.m.

He carried wood from the forest, trudged through the sand, and stacked it by the fire. Night was falling and the temperature had dropped several degrees with the sun. He threw a few logs into the mix to bring the flames back to life and warm his body. He didn't have much fat to protect him from the elements, and his clothing had seen better days. When the fire was raging and self-sufficient, he sat in the chair outside his shack. He pulled the journal from the backpack, thumbed the pages to where he had left off, and allowed the flames to brighten the page as he read the heading:

The Day You Were Born

I sat next to Abby as she lay in the hospital, propped up by pillows. You had been born hours earlier, and we still had not held you. Abby's obstetrician stood at the foot of the bed and another, unfamiliar doctor waited suspiciously in the background.

"Immediately after delivery," our doctor said,

"I noticed Jacob's skin color was abnormal, and he was not responding to his surroundings. That's why we brought him so quickly to the neonatal intensive care unit. Jacob's initial symptoms were consistent with sepsis, a blood infection that is undetectable in vitro but which has a distinct clinical appearance upon birth. However, he didn't respond to antibiotic therapy, so we ran more tests. This is Dr. Harding. She's a pediatric oncologist who will explain what we've found."

The title of oncologist *sent my insides tumbling.*

The specialist introduced herself. Even before she spoke, though, her eyes gave too much away.

"When Jacob didn't respond to antibiotic therapy, I examined his blood cells, as well as his bone marrow. The tests revealed atypical cells consistent with acute myeloid leukemia, or what's generically referred to as congenital leukemia."

I felt Abby's hand squeeze my own.

"What does it mean?" I asked. "How do you treat it?"

"I'm going to do everything possible for your son, but . . ." She paused, searching for words. "I'm afraid the prognosis in these cases is poor. We can consider chemotherapy, and we'll go over the specifics if you choose that route. However, I've looked closely at Jacob's smears and his is a severe case. I don't believe treatment will have a beneficial effect. I'm being blunt because it's important for you to understand what's happening. It's important to prepare yourselves."

"Prepare ourselves for what?" Abby asked in a feeble voice.

"Only a small minority of congenital leukemia patients survives beyond twenty-four months."

I swallowed hard and tried not to look at Abby.
"There's no way to fix this?" I asked.
"I'm afraid not."

Ben closed the journal as he looked back to the fire. The sky was dark now, with just a glowing blue ribbon left on the horizon. He ran a hand over the cover of the journal as a tear traced down his cheek until his beard absorbed it. When he heard the door of the kid's shack, just twenty yards from his own, open, he wiped his cheek.

Ben cleared his throat. "William," he said as the teenager walked over and stood by the fire.

The kid lifted his hand in a gentle wave and then pointed at the journal. "How'd I do?"

"It's perfect, every page. Thank you again. It would have been ruined if you hadn't taken care of it."

"It seems like the journal means a lot to you."

"It does. It contains a series of letters I wrote to my son, Jacob."

Ben walked over and joined William by the fire.

"Really. That journal means the world to me, and I'm very grateful you found it."

"It's the least I can do," William said. "Considering everything you're doing for me and my dad."

The two had been through a great deal together, and although theirs was an unlikely alliance formed out of necessity and survival, it had developed into a loyal friendship.

Ben pointed at William's shack. "How's your dad doing?"

William shook his head. "Today's a bad day."

"I wish I could do more for him."

"You can," William said. "We have a plan for how to help him. We just need to stick to it."

Ben nodded as he looked past the fire and toward the dark ocean in front of them.

"I'll stick to it. It's a promise," he said.

Chapter 13

The Decision

Friday, April 14
6:45 a.m.

The winter had been harsh but was finally beginning to fade. Spring was here—not quite visible in the trees or landscape but tangible in the way the air felt and smelled. Parkas had been exchanged for windbreakers. Gloves and hats were stowed. The days stretched longer, and the sun lasted deeper into evening. Warm air thawed frost from the ground in hazy spells of morning fog. Tulips pushed through the earth, geese bawled early in the morning, and for the first time in nearly a year, when the morning sun was soft on her pillow, Abby Gamble woke without the torment of her husband's absence weighing on her mind.

Time was the healer of all ailments—slight, sometimes indiscernible, progress happened every day until the cumulative effect was the small victory of waking without sadness. It was a welcomed relief from the first few months, which had felt like a difficult climb up a steep bank, each step more arduous than the last. The recovery of Ben's watch and wallet had been the pinnacle of her grief. It was proof, as much as on track. Something had changed inside her since the anguish of Christmas. Like a car being overdriven in third gear and suddenly shifting to fourth, daily events were easier and less strained. She couldn't explain what it was or how it happened. Things just felt easier. Where before her memories were like picking through shattered glass, choosing the pieces that seemed safe and avoiding the shards that could cut, Abby now found herself able to frolic in her memories of Ben. Imagining his face and feeling the power of his smile helped her accept that he was in a better place. Somewhere safe and spectacular, and any pain he might have endured in the moments before he made it to this special place was gone and vanished. It was the only thing she *could* imagine because the alternative had been ruining her. She decided Ben wouldn't want that for her. She decided that Ben would want her to move on and be free from heartache, and for the first time Abby sensed that walking away from the anguish of losing her husband was something that might be possible.

As her grief faded, her thoughts turned to Jacob. Not a single day had gone by in the previous twelve years when Abby did not think of her son. But in the first months after Ben's death her heart had no room for the extra pain and could not sustain the added weight of another burden, and so thoughts of Jacob had faded into the background. She felt guilty for keeping her son absent from her thoughts for so long. Unlike the memories of Ben, twelve years had softened the blow of losing Jacob, and when Abby thought of her son she did so with pride and jubilation. Of course, it hadn't always been that way. Jacob's death had produced an anguish that seeped into her heart the way a decades-old bottle of wine works its way into the cork that holds it. But when tears came now, they were not because she missed him, but because she never got to know him. Never got to see his first step or hear his first word or witness his first smile. Never got to see him score a goal or throw a touchdown. She often pictured Jacob in her mind. Thinking of what he would look like now. Imagining what his voice would sound like, and the type of young man he would be.

Her mind drifted to the day her son was taken from this world. She sat in the hospital chair, Ben's arms around her, wrapped tight. Hers around Jacob. The tubes that fed life to their son had been removed after three long months. The *whish-woo* of the ventilator was gone and a strange silence filled the room. She'd cried in free-fall that day, no end in sight. She remembered the feeling of Ben's tears on her neck when they both knew it was over. Their decision to donate Jacob's organs was an effort to make sense of the senseless and assign meaning to his short life. If Jacob could help other sick children, his short time on this planet would be worth the pain she and Ben were enduring. But that decision added a timeline to the end of Jacob's life, and medical staff waited patiently for them to relinquish their child after he passed. Two days later, the funeral cut her down to nothing, and a year of anguish followed. It was much like the past year that Abby had endured.

During the year after Jacob's death, she and Ben worked and slept. They rarely talked about their son—their hearts ached too much to do so—and because they thought of little else, they stopped talking entirely, both locked in their own world of pain and penance, unable to help themselves or each other. It was a dangerous year for their marriage. They lost their intimacy and damaged their bond as they each dealt with a grief never before encountered. A grief whose weight and presence was so immense that it threatened to produce a sinkhole that swallowed them both.

They had refused the help of those who extended it to them. Grief counseling was shunned. Family members ignored. Sundays at church—which had been a part of each of their lives before they met and had grown into a weekly strengthening of both their faith and love during their time together—had ended. Even the secret visits Abby made to her minister eventually wound down. Then, on what would have been Jacob's first birthday, they uttered their first words about him in many months.

"Do you know what today is?" Abby asked while they were readying for work.

It was early morning, and both had showered. They were staring into the bathroom mirror. Both were lost and alone, barely recognizing the couple that stared back. But that morning they would find each other, two isolated drifters coming together at just the right time. Their paths somehow crossing as they each blindly roamed.

"His birthday," Ben said, moving his gaze to meet his wife's.

Abby's eyes filled with tears, her bottom lip quivered. In an instant they moved to one another. They held each other tightly, each finding relief in the other's touch. She cried, as hard as she had the year before.

"I want him back," Ben said into her ear. "We lost him, and I want him back."

She took his face in her hands and looked into his eyes. "We can't get him back, Ben. We've spent a year refusing to believe this, and it's killing us. It's ruining who we are, and now it's time to decide. We either let it kill us, or we overcome it. One or the other."

"I miss him."

"Me too," Abby said. "So much."

Neither made it to work that day, or for a month after. They found a secluded house a thousand miles away, in Lake Tahoe, and spent four weeks rejuvenating their relationship and tending to wounds they had ignored for a year. They made love for the first time in months, and as they experienced the joy of falling in love again, the pain from losing their son began to seep into the past.

It was those weeks together, Abby remembered, that saved her marriage. It was those four weeks that saved her life. As she pushed the covers to the side and stood from her bed nearly one year after Ben had died, she thought that she again needed an intervention. That her life needed saving, just like before.

It was time to decide. She could either let the pain of Ben's death kill her, or she could overcome it.

Chapter 14

A Confession

Saturday, April 15
10:32 a.m.

*T*he journey was uphill. The rocks into which the end of
the log was jammed pitched it up at a slight angle as they
ventured farther along the trunk with the river moving fast
beneath them. When they made it to the rocks they both sat
cowboy-style with the log between their legs, their feet dan-
gling on either side. Joel's legs were too short for his shoes to
touch the water, but as the two boys settled themselves onto
the wood, the river reached up and sucked his brother's right
sneaker from his foot.

"Damn! There goes my Chuck Taylor."

They both watched as the canvas high-top rode the rapids,
bounced off a rock, and disappeared. The missing shoe
would be impossible to explain to their father.

"Maybe we should go back," Joel said. The river suddenly
looked more dangerous than ever before.

His brother looked upriver to the overpass. "No time.
Come on. Let's get up on the rocks."

With both hands between their legs, they scooted forward

*on the seat of their pants until they came to the twin boul-
ders. Joel's brother climbed on top of one, placing most of his
weight on his remaining shoe. Joel mimicked his brother's
motion and climbed opposite him on the other rock. They
each examined the fallen trunk that was their escape to the
other side of the river. But the rotten wood was farther from
the rocks than it had appeared when they studied it from the
bank.*

*The evening sun was low and cast the tree trunks in long
shadows across the river. Their own shadows fell like ghosts
onto the water below. Their father had taught them compass
settings based on which way the shadows stretched and what
time of day it was. The river ran north and south, and the
thin outline of their bodies bled from their feet, across the
felled trunk, and nearly to the bank on the other side. They
were facing east, and both Keaton boys wished they could
make it to the riverbank as easily as their shadows.*

"I'll go first," Joel's brother said

"What if I can't make it and you're gone?" Joel asked.

*Joel watched as his brother contemplated his argument. It
would be a tough jump the first time around, and the last
thing his brother would want was to have to make it twice:
once for himself and a second time to retrieve Joel.*

*"Okay," Joel's brother finally said. "You go first. I'll fol-
low you. Here's what you do: Get yourself all the way to the
edge of your rock, then jump for that dry spot." He pointed
to the tree trunk. "See it?"*

"Yeah."

"If you hit the wet spot, you're gonna fall in."

"Okay," Joel said, eying the landing area.

"Hurry. Dad'll be home soon."

*Joel moved to the edge of the rock and squatted until the
seat of his pants touched the granite, then rose slowly and
jumped. The rubber bottoms of his shoes met the dry bark of*

the felled tree, and after two adjustment steps, he righted himself. He turned and squatted, holding the trunk for balance. He smiled at his older brother and pumped his fist. There would be great stories to tell.

His brother moved to the edge of his own rock. Water surged below them, and Joel felt the spray on his face. The roar of the river filled his ears as he watched his brother bend his knees and prepare to jump. He looked awkward and uncomfortable with only one shoe. Joel's brother held up his index finger first, then his middle finger, and finally his ring finger. Joel made the three-count in his mind: One. Two. Three!

His brother lunged from the rock, but his bare foot slipped and deflected off the granite as he jumped. He barely made it halfway to Joel. Even his fully outstretched arms couldn't reach the safety of the trunk before his body hit the water. As if he were clutching and crawling along a slick hardwood floor, the river pulled him against his will. His body found the same rock as his Chuck Taylor had a few minutes earlier, the water punching him hard into the stone and then climbing over his head. The fierce eddy currents and undertow eventually spun him around and spit him out past the rock, where the main current then dragged him farther down river. He came to another fallen trunk and managed to get his arms around it, his body strung out horizontally as the water pulled him. He lost his other shoe. His shorts slipped down by his thighs until, thirty seconds later, they were gone.

He was only twenty yards from the rocks where he and Joel had jumped, but it may as well have been a mile. As his brother clung to the log, Joel heard him yell over the roar of the river.

"Get help!"

"What?"

"Get Brandon!" his brother yelled. "Hurry!"

Joel turned and ran along the trunk, jumping onto solid ground. He ran down river until he was parallel to his brother. "I'll go home and get Mom."

"No! Get Brandon! Hurry!"

Joel turned and ran.

Joel Keaton sat by the bedside, eyes closed, the raging river and his older brother's cries for help echoing in his ears. The monitors rhythmically beeped, and this far into his father's illness Joel had become deaf to the gauges and devices that told him how close his father was to death.

He sat upright in the chair and then leaned toward his father.

"Dad."

There was no response.

"Dad, can you hear me?"

Joel saw a subtle nod from his father, but his eyes remained closed and his mouth frozen, with cracked lips parted in the motionless way Joel had seen so many times over the course of his career. Death was coming.

"Dad, I have to tell you something. It's about the river. I've kept it a secret too long."

A slight burst of adrenaline raised his father's eyelids for a brief moment. Joel knew he had his father's attention—as much of it as was possible for a man who was so close to death.

"I know what happened. I was there."

Chapter 15

Girls' Night Out

Saturday, April 15
7:25 p.m.

At thirty-four, Abby still had that immaculate look of youth—a wrinkle-free face with unblemished skin that easily fought the dragging effects of gravity. When she smiled, a dimple formed on her right cheek—a characteristic that was always described as *cute*, which she'd hated when she was younger but now, in her thirties, appreciated. She grabbed her purse when she heard the cab's horn and headed out the door for her first social night out in almost a year. She had decided to get her life back on track, and doing so with her sister felt like the right way to start. Dinner and drinks with her younger sister had been a regular occurrence before Ben's death, and with her self-administered intervention underway, Abby decided the first step would be welcoming her sister back into her life.

When she exited her townhouse, she found Maggie waiting by the cab, the back passenger-side door open, and a smile across her face. She held up her hands, each filled with Yetis clinking with the muffled sound of ice cubes.

"Let's go, sister," Maggie said.

"What do you have there?" Abby asked as she walked down the steps.

"Margaritas. Strawberry."

"You can't take those in a cab."

"I just did. Call the cops," Maggie said as she slid into the back seat.

Abby shook her head and couldn't help but smile. She'd missed her sister.

"Pops for Champagne," Maggie said to the driver. "On Sheffield."

As the cab took off from the curb Maggie handed Abby a margarita.

"Have you gone mad?" Abby asked.

"What do you mean?"

"Margaritas in the back of a cab? How old are we?"

"I'm twenty-nine," Maggie said, taking a sip. "If you want me to bark out your age, I'll go right ahead. But I'd keep that under wraps."

"You're *thirty*, and what's gotten into you?"

"I'm excited. We haven't been out in a long time."

"Don't get your hopes up. I'll probably be falling asleep by ten."

"Oh, come on. We're going to have fun."

The cab pulled to the curb in front of Pops, a trendy wine bar for the thirty-something crowd. Inside, several round tables scattered throughout the lounge area were arranged for groups of two or four, with white tablecloths that hung midway to the floor. A grand piano sat on a slightly elevated stage where guest musicians played seven nights a week.

Pops was crowded that night. A waitress took their drink orders after they were seated—two brut rosé champagnes served in tall, fluted glasses. They talked for an hour, catching up on each other's lives. They talked through two drinks and when the third arrived, Maggie looked at her older sister with a more serious expression.

"Abby, I've got something to tell you . . ."

"What's wrong?"

"Nothing, it's just that . . ." Maggie forced a smile.

"Who's sick?"

"No one."

"Did Mom and Dad have another breakdown about me?"

"No. It's nothing like that. It's just that . . ."

Abby waited.

". . . Jim and I are trying for a baby."

Abby stared for a second with squinted eyes. There was a bloated moment where the sisters looked at each other, then Abby pulled Maggie's fluted glass away from her. "Are you crazy? You can't drink champagne. What if you're already pregnant?"

Maggie laughed. "We're not trying *yet*. I ovulate in two weeks. Twelve days, to be precise, if the damn thermometer is correct."

"Oh," Abby said, handing the champagne back to Maggie. "Then what's the problem? We should be celebrating."

"Yeah, well, I wasn't sure, you know, if you wanted to know about it."

"Are you kidding? I want to know everything. I mean, leave the conception out, but everything else I want to hear about." Abby shook her head. "My kid sister, having a baby. I still think of you as a little girl, and now you're ready to have a baby. Whatever happened to those two little girls? Little Abigail and Margaret Hartland?"

"All grown up, I guess."

The waitress approached with two tall glasses of champagne. "These are compliments of the gentlemen at the bar," the waitress said. She set the drinks on the table and left.

Slowly, Abby and Maggie moved their eyes—which had

for the last several seconds been slightly widened and fixed at each other's—toward the bar, until they saw two guys staring at them. They were good-looking. One had an oxford shirt open at the collar; the other was wearing a stockbroker sport jacket over a blue button-down. The men raised their glasses as soon as Abby and Maggie's eyes reached them.

The sisters broke into a huddled laugh, embarrassed and flattered. Then Maggie stiffened and collected herself before turning back to the men and raising her drink.

"Cheers," she yelled over the piano music.

The men smiled and tilted their glasses toward them.

"Should we ask them over?" Maggie asked.

Abby squinted her eyes at her younger sister. "For Christ's sake, Maggie. We're married."

As soon as Abby spoke the words she stopped and stared at the table, the smile falling from her face as she realized her mistake.

"You're right," Maggie said. "It's not a good idea."

"No. It's fine. It's just that . . . I'm not . . . you know . . ."

"Fried shrimp!" Maggie said, deadpan and staring Abby straight in the face.

"What?"

"We haven't figured out where we're going for dinner yet. How about fried shrimp?"

Abby closed her eyes and smiled. They had always had that inverse relationship—Maggie, the younger sister, was the one who did the protecting.

"That sounds great."

"Good. There's a seafood place down the block. If we go now there probably won't be a wait."

They paid their bill and were on the way out a minute later. Maggie gave the guys a wink on the way past.

"Thanks for the drinks, fellas."

* * *

Later that night, Abby found herself back in the familiar nook of her couch, lights dimmed, the box of greeting cards and letters next to her. They had become a strange crutch she used to limp through intermittent stages of pain. She knew it was unhealthy, but the ache was with her again that night, since she had said good-bye to Maggie.

It had happened before, and she'd never minded attention from other men. She'd always found it flattering. But this was the first time she had received that attention since losing him. The first time she couldn't flash her ring as a way out. The night she realized she was no longer married.

Twelve years of marriage and three years of dating added up to a decade and a half of commitment; not something easily discarded, and without which she felt naked. But in that feeling of emptiness, Abby also realized the void would never be filled if she refused to move forward.

She stared at her wedding ring, firmly affixed to her left ring finger. She twirled it slightly, cracking it free from the crater it rested in. She spun it in circles for a minute and almost pulled it over her knuckle. Eventually, though, she stopped fiddling with it and instead replaced the cards and letters neatly in the box. She stared at them for a moment before she closed the lid and climbed the stairs to her bedroom. She stored the box back on the top shelf of the closet from which she had retrieved it on Christmas Eve, then walked to the dresser and looked at Ben's wallet and watch, still waiting, as if he might return. Abby took the watch and examined it. It had been a present for Ben's thirtieth birthday—a Rolex that cost too much and was a sign of their rising affluence. Over the course of the previous week or two it had stopped ticking. She picked up his wallet and inspected the contents, stopping at Ben's driver's license. She looked at the photo and thumbed a smudge off the laminated surface. Finally she made her way to the small step stool in the closet.

Hesitant at first but forcing herself on, she climbed up two steps and placed her husband's watch and wallet into the box that held the cards and letters he had written to her. She closed the lid and ran her hand over the top.

She hit the light switch on the way out of the closet, casting into darkness her memories of the only man she had ever loved.

Chapter 16

The Nose

Sunday, April 16
7:22 a.m.

The rain forest was dark and quiet early in the morning, except for the sound of water running through the stream, curling around rocks and swelling over fallen bamboo as it twisted its way through the island. Ben followed its current until it led him to the giant red cedar. When he first found the tree, a thin vine had just blossomed at its base, but months later, the vine crawled halfway up the trunk. It was a barren vine, free of branches or sprouts, but it was growing rapidly. It encircled the broad trunk and over the previous few weeks had begun to partially cover his artwork.

He felt a strange but comforting connection to this tree, drawn to its strength and shelter. He came here daily, if for no other reason than to stay on track. It kept him focused. A patch of bark was missing along the surface of the trunk, and he rubbed his hand over the smooth wood that was exposed. From his pocket he removed the Swiss Army knife, unfolded the blade, and pressed the tip into the tree trunk. He whittled another small mark into the wood. It joined the hundreds of others he had made—short, vertical bars organized in clusters of five. He counted them again. Three hundred thirty-five in all, one for every day he'd been there.

He studied his handiwork for a moment longer, then turned from the tree, walked out of the forest and into the clearing. The stream he had been following drained into a vast lagoon, the water of which was ice blue, calm and unmoving that morning. Now that he was out of the canopied forest, the sky unfolded above him in a network of charcoal-grey clouds. Another storm was coming.

He looked across the lagoon. It was there, on the opposite shore, where the fuselage of the airplane had come to rest. The front section of the plane was pitched at a downward angle that submerged the nose beneath the surface of the water. Jagged shards of metal, where the plane had been torn in half, stuck up into the air. He closed his eyes and remembered the view out his window just before impact, when the water rose up to meet the plane. The screams of the passengers still echoed in his ears, and worse, the eerie silence that followed as water filled the cabin. Ben couldn't remember much after that. When he'd first crawled his way onto shore near the lagoon, he believed he was the only one who had survived, and that no other soul was on the island. Then he found William.

Next to the wreckage, and scattered around the lagoon, were the shacks he and William had discovered when they first explored the island together. The small structures offered shelter from the storms that often assaulted the island. For the last several months Ben had made one of those shacks his home. But it was only temporary, he continued to remind himself. The hash marks he carved into the tree were more than a way to keep track of the days. They were a promise to himself that no matter how many days went by, he'd find his way back to Abby. Thoughts of her had gotten him this far, and he'd never give up hope that he'd see her again.

Three hundred thirty-five days. As Ben pulled the straps of the Gore-Tex backpack tight onto his shoulders, he headed toward the wreckage and wondered how many more days it would be until he'd see his wife again.

Chapter 17

The Secret

Sunday, April 16
8:32 p.m.

The woman pulled her car to the curb in front of the house and watched Ben Gamble's widow climb the porch stairs and walk through the front door. She watched for some time, seeing the house come to life as lights clicked on. She worked hard to find the courage to exit her car, walk up the steps, and knock on the front door. As usual, though, despite her efforts, she couldn't gather the strength. Instead, she pulled the letter from her pocket and read it in the soft glow of the car's dome light.

> *Hi,*
> *I know I have to tell Abby about everything. I'm planning to, I promise. But the timing is not right. I need more time to figure things out. To make sure this is the right thing to do. You and I didn't plan this, it just happened. It's still a surprise to me, and I need some time to figure out how to tell her. I don't want to*

*hurt her, and I know you understand. Please give me
that time—just a little longer.*
   I'm excited to see you both this weekend.
                        —Ben

A year had passed since Ben's plane went down. She was lost during the first few months, alone with their secret. But now, nearly a year later, she needed to speak with Abby Gamble. There was simply no way around it. She couldn't keep this secret any longer.

An hour passed as she sat in the car. Ben's house slowly fell into darkness as his wife moved from room to room shutting off the lights until only the bedroom window glowed. When, finally, that window too went dark, the woman folded Ben's letter and placed it in her purse. She had many more she planned to show his widow. She turned and reached into the back seat, checking to make sure the child was fastened securely in his car seat. She was a nervous mother, always fearful that something terrible would happen to her child. Once she heard the soft murmur of his breathing, she clicked off the dome light, shifted the car into gear, and pulled slowly from the curb.

She'd come back another time. Perhaps then she'd find the courage to tell Abby Gamble about the secret she shared with Abby's husband.

PART III

FINDING HIM

Chapter 18

Washing Hands

Tuesday, May 2
3:32 p.m.

*T*he long black Mercedes Benz was in the driveway when Joel sprinted around the corner. This was a problem. His father was home. He quickly formulated a plan to sneak through the back door, tiptoe past his father's den, and then race upstairs. He would tell Brandon everything and they would hurry back to the river. To hell with dinner, they would think of an excuse.

Joel muffled the squeak of the screen door by opening it slowly, a change from the frantic pace his body had taken for the mile-and-a-half hike home from the river. He had cut through backyards and over fences, raced over the graves of Gentry Cemetery and made record time. He was sweaty and out of breath and worked to control his wheezing lungs as he sneaked into the house. The den was empty, his first bit of luck. Up the back stairs without a hitch and down the hall-way to Brandon's room. Empty. Joel checked the bathroom. No luck. He began to fidget with his fingers as indecision descended. He heard the clinking of dinner plates in the kitchen *and then the deep voice of his adolescent brother. Brandon's voice had taken on that adult tone over the last few months, and Joel wanted to crawl right up into it and ask for help. He needed Brandon in the worst way.*

He heard the door to the patio slide open and his mother's voice fade as she walked outside, probably to talk with his father, who was likely sitting as usual with legs crossed and drinking a tumbler full of the brown liquid Joel had sipped one time. It had burned his throat and made his eyes water. Now, he knew, was his only chance.

The stairs were handled in seconds, and he stormed into the kitchen to find Brandon sitting at the dinner table reading a comic book. His sister, Rachel, was setting the table for dinner. Joel had his sentence planned out, about how they tried to cross the river but it was too high, and now their brother was clinging to a log and only Brandon could help and they had to go now! Right now, this very minute, because he wouldn't be able to hold on to that log much longer . . .

But before Joel could start the sentence, his father walked into the kitchen. The tumbler in his hand was empty, and he stared at Joel with narrowed eyes and a look of suspicion across his face.

"Clean your hands and get ready for dinner," his father said.

Joel stared at Brandon with panicked eyes that caused his older brother to laugh.

"What's wrong with you?" Brandon said. "Clean your hands."

"Yeah," Rachel said. His little sister's voice was high and childlike compared to Brandon's. "Your hands are all dirty."

For a suspended moment, the sentence Joel had prepared sat on the tip of his tongue and nearly slipped out. He wanted to cough it up and vomit it into the kitchen so it was out there and he couldn't take it back. For a second, he wanted his father's wrath for going to the river, because that would mean he'd also have his help. But that second passed, and then another and another. Inexplicably, Joel slowly walked to the sink and lathered his hands.

The bristles of the surgical brush scraped over the nails and cuticles of Dr. Joel Keaton's fingers as he stood in front of the scrub sink. It was always a work of penance to lather his hands before surgery—the routine took him back to the night he left his brother to die at the river while he washed his hands in the kitchen sink instead of asking for his father's help. That nearly thirty years had passed hadn't softened the guilt of that day; that he had never shared his secret added to it.

Since that moment at the kitchen sink, Joel's secret had tainted his relationship with both his father and Brandon. In the days after the drowning, his father asked Brandon a hundred times about the river, and whether he had ever taken his two young brothers there. Brandon's denials never seemed to satisfy their father. How could they? Brandon had taken his younger brothers to the river on dozens of occasions, and the three Keaton boys had climbed across that river too many times to count. But it was Brandon who had always warned his little brothers about the dangers of crossing the river when it was high, and it was only when the two youngest Keaton boys had ventured there on their own that things had gone wrong. Joel's father never came right out and blamed Brandon for what happened, but the unspoken suspicion was worse than the accusation itself. That Joel knew the truth and kept it to himself was a burden that weighed him down the remainder of his childhood. His secret destroyed the brotherly bond he'd shared with Brandon, who had his own suspicions about that day. And it caused a breach in his relationship with his father that could never be bridged.

Joel had tried a number of things to blunt the destructive effects of his secret and put off the chore of facing it head-on. During his teen years, he turned in on himself and became a recluse. Rejecting the love of those around him seemed a small price to pay for his sins. The habit continued into adulthood and was especially profound when it came to allowing himself to love a woman. Self-sabotage was a common theme in Joel Keaton's love life. As an adult, he buried himself in the rigors of medical school and residency and then later allowed his career to consume him. He had never wanted to be a doctor; that was his brother's dream. But becoming a surgeon served as a way to win favor with a father who was never the same after the police officer stood on the front porch to tell him his middle son had drowned in the Pichatauk River. That Joel had grown into a gifted surgeon—the vocation his dead brother had hoped to pursue—was both a curse Joel had learned to live with, and an irony that could never be explained. Washing his hands under the watchful eye of his father thirty years earlier had cost his brother's life; now, that same action represented salvation to those who waited for the touch of his gifted hands.

Joel took a deep breath and let the hot water rinse away the soap and memories and guilt, hoping his anxiety would spin down the drain as well. He'd performed the procedure one thousand three hundred seventeen times in his thirteen years of surgery. An appendectomy was as straightforward as they came. But still the butterflies fluttered in his stomach, a sensation he had never before encountered during his career. Unlike his fellow residents who stood with shaking hands before their first cut, Joel had never found fear in surgery. His success was not for himself, but for the brother he had failed. He allowed neither trepidation nor sympathy to interfere with his objective or alter his judgment.

He had allowed fear to hold him back once before—as a

ten-year-old, when his brother needed him most. Although Joel lost his brother that day, a kindred friendship continued between them. In the quiet recesses of his mind Joel promised his brother that he would never again allow fear to stop him from saving a life. The promise was Joel's apology for failing his brother, and in some transcendent way, Joel felt that mastering medicine was the best way to honor his brother.

As his career progressed, Joel saw colleagues devastated by lost patients and unfair cases. It was never fair when a kid died. Or when a drunk driver found a father of four on a dark road in the middle of the night. But those were the tragedies of medicine and life, and becoming emotionally attached to patients was a mistake lesser surgeons made. Joel had never fallen prey to the illusion that if a surgeon cared more they would do a better job. He performed best with a clear mind unclouded by sentiment. "Get 'em in, get 'em open, get 'em out," his mentor used to tell him. "But get to know 'em on your own time."

As he looked through the window of the operating room doors now, however, he stared at his nephew lying on the table and found he was not only emotionally involved, but nervous as hell. He had paged a few other general surgeons on staff. The first two were out of town, the third was tied up in surgery, and the fourth was an hour away at his kid's basketball game. With Brian running a high fever, an hour was too long. So for the first time in his career, Joel Keaton entered the OR with a brow soaked in perspiration and hands that were less than steady.

"Should I adjust the air-conditioning, Dr. Keaton?" the scrub nurse asked as she held a surgical glove wide for Joel to snake his hand into.

"Do what?"

"The air-conditioning. Make it cooler?" She pointed to his forehead. "You're sweating."

"Oh," Joel said, letting the words register. "Yes. Please."

He shoved his hand into the waiting glove and flexed his fingers. Then the other glove before he turned for the nurse to tie his gown. He approached the table where the resident was prepping Brian's abdomen. Normally, Joel would allow the third-year resident to open and close. But not tonight. Not with Brian.

"I've got this one," Joel said. He studied the prep job and found no flaws. With his eyes focused on the brown Betadine covering his nephew's skin, he visualized the procedure. It was his routine, something he never strayed from. Something he never taught either, unable to explain to respected colleagues, let alone wide-eyed residents, how his mind ran through procedures—sometimes hours long—in just seconds, missing no details. As soon as he held the scalpel in his hand and made a three-inch incision in the lower right quadrant of his nephew's abdomen, his hands and fingers relaxed and moved in a smooth rhythm. The blade glided through the skin and subcutaneous fat. The muscle of the abdominal wall separated without protest under the pressure of the scalpel. Once he was lost in the anatomy, the nervousness and apprehension drifted away slowly and without notice, the way an unsecured boat floats from shore. He slipped into cruise control, and although no one in the room noticed the transformation, he felt it, as he morphed silently from a worried uncle into the skilled surgeon he was. The Denver-Wells retractors widened the incision, and he marked the cecum of the large intestine as his landmark, then studied the small intestine until he found the appendix. It was edematous and hot, and Joel figured he had gotten to it just before it ruptured.

Thirty minutes into the procedure, it was nearly over. Brian's appendix—an ugly piece of tissue that resembled a small porterhouse—lay on a metal tray next to the table. Joel began a cursory search of Brian's abdomen to make sure no surgical instruments or gauze pads were left behind. He was an old-school cutter who preferred traditional surgery with an open approach, versus laparoscopy. On this day he was especially happy about it. He might have missed it had he used the scope. But with Brian's abdomen open, Joel had a better view of the organs, and that was how he found it. He had removed enough cancerous tumors in his career to know one immediately. And there it sat, attached to Brian's peritoneum. The sweat returned to his forehead.

"I think I see a mass here. I need to do some exploration." Joel widened the incision and let his mind take over, rising like an incoming tide over his fear. "Call oncology and get Bill Blakely on the phone." He looked up at his nurse. "Do it now, please."

The nurse was back two minutes later with the OR phone wrapped with a sterile pack. She held it to Joel's ear. "Hey, Bill, Joel Keaton. I've got a twelve-year-old male. Uncomplicated appendectomy. Secondarily, I noticed what looks like a mesothelioma, about three-and-a-half inches around. It's a personal case for me and I was hoping you could run over and take a look . . . okay . . . will do."

Joel delicately removed the mass, peeling it away from the abdominal cavity and cauterizing the feeder vessels as he proceeded. By the time Bill Blakely, the head of surgical oncology, scrubbed in, the growth lay on the metal specimen tray. It was ugly and dead, and Joel knew too well that masses like that could leave patients the same way. There was something there he hated—a sense of helplessness and failure in the blood-covered tissue he'd removed. Something he couldn't control. The growth, worthless and mangled now, may have already injected its deadly touch into his young nephew's body, and it was beyond the healing touch his own hands were capable of delivering.

Dr. Blakely searched for thirty minutes but found no other

masses. His face carried the stoic look of a surgeon working on a stranger. Joel recognized the expression from years of carrying it himself. Dr. Blakely dissected and removed the appropriate lymph nodes and excised small samples for biopsy from surrounding organs. They sent the tumor, tissue, and nodes to pathology while Joel closed Brian's abdomen.

He would put some pressure on pathology the next day, and by afternoon they would know more about Brian's prognosis. Know if it was a metastasis. Know if the lymph nodes were involved. Know if his nephew had a chance or if a silent killer had sneaked into his body and taken firm command of how things would progress.

Joel left the OR and found his sister in the waiting room. Rachel had been through so much with Brian already and had dodged so many bullets in the last twelve years that it was hard to fathom escaping another. Joel sat with his sister, holding her hand and wiping her tears and wondering if every parent didn't deserve the same time and sympathy. He wondered why he had never offered his other patients the same compassion. He'd opened abdomens in the past only to close them back up a minute later after seeing cancer pocked over the organs with such rancid aggression that there was no hope that anything he could do would stop death from coming. His explanation to the relatives of these patients had scarcely lasted five minutes, the case forgotten but for the occasional worst-case comparisons between colleagues.

Get 'em in, get 'em open, get 'em out. Help 'em when you can but don't beat yourself up when you can't.

There was a reason Joel was bad at this part of his job. Delivering terrible news to the relatives always brought him back to the day the police officer stood on the front porch of his childhood home and broke the news to his father. When family members wept, Joel remembered seeing his father that day, a pillar of strength, cry for the first time—crumbling to one knee as he heard that his son had drowned. Throughout his career Joel had made himself numb to the emotions patients and family displayed in the face of bad news. To do anything else would put him back thirty years, and he had spent too much time dwelling there during the small hours of night to retreat to the same place during his waking hours.

He pushed from his mind the memories of his brother and the river, his guilt-riddled childhood and the landmines that could at any moment trigger an explosion of remorse, and made sure to be present for Rachel, who cried on his shoulder as he held her tight.

Two hours after he'd left Rachel sitting at Brian's bedside, Joel walked into the hospice facility and took his own spot next to a different patient. His father lay unmoving, his chest rising every few seconds with labored breathing.

It had never been a formulated plan to take to his grave the secret about the day his brother died at the river. Joel had never fully worked it out in his mind that he would forever hide the details of that day; it was just the way his life had taken shape. He'd said nothing that night and stayed silent in the days after his brother's body was discovered. One day led to another, and then another, until months and then years had passed. Eventually so much time had gone by that the secret became part of him. There were many times when the weight of his silence had become too much to bear and when Joel thought of telling his father what had happened that day at the river. But then he would reconsider. To unearth the truth so suddenly, years later and out of context, would only reopen old wounds. But now, as his father approached death, Joel decided that he couldn't allow him to leave this world without knowing what had happened to his son that afternoon. Whether by choice or circumstance, the time for the truth had come.

Joel took his father's hand.

"Dad?"

There was no indication that his father heard him, but that didn't stop Joel from speaking.

"I was there that day. At the river. I could have saved him, but I was too scared. I'm sorry I never told you what happened. But I want to tell you now . . ."

His father's eyes opened, and on a cool spring night, a man burdened by a lifelong secret confessed to his dying father the role he'd played in the death of his older brother thirty years before.

Chapter 19

Clammy Hands

Friday, May 5
7:12 p.m.

The Drake Hotel sat just off the banks of Lake Michigan, across eight lanes of Lake Shore Drive, and had been standing since Woodrow Wilson occupied the White House. The interior, although modern, held the stately look of years ago. The Venetian Room was set for one hundred twenty-five guests. A score of round tables filled the room and were covered with formal dinnerware; a long rectangular head table would hold the distinguished guest speakers. A large screen hung from the ceiling in the corner and caught the blue light from the projector. A few eager physicians milled around and pored over the program, finding their seats and getting an early word with the gurus who would give the presentation and offer their expertise. The topic was gastric bypass, a procedure whose popularity was skyrocketing under the discovery of new and safer techniques.

Joel Keaton stood downstairs in the lobby, pacing between a couch in the lounge and the men's room. He took a deep breath. It had been a long time since he'd done this. He had structured his life in a way that rarely had him out of sorts or placed him outside his comfort zone. Even when he ventured into the unknown in his occupation, he did so in the controlled environment of the operating room. He could do anything there, when he was focused and headed toward a definite solution. But tonight was something different. Tonight he was not only out of his comfort zone, he was in a different zip code entirely. He had no idea where he was headed or how the night would end, and the uncertainty had his stomach in a knot. His hands were clammy, and his pacing was adding to his anxiety.

But something happened when he spotted her. She was dressed in a black gown, which hung delicately just above her knees. As she walked, her heels propped her up and gave way to toned calves, which carried a tan that had no business in Chicago this early in spring. The last finger of winter had lost its grip a few weeks back, and she wore a shawl over her shoulders to keep at bay the bite that remained in the air. Her auburn hair was up and pulled back, a single strand falling to the side of her face, accenting her bronzed skin, which was tight and youthful.

Her face broke into a wide smile when she saw him, and that was all it took. Her smile did something to him, shifted some unknown lever in his nervous system that allowed him to find the comfort and confidence that usually guided his life. As he walked toward her, his hands dried up and his stomach settled. He met her with a light kiss on the cheek.

"You look gorgeous."

"Thank you." She smiled, looking him up and down. "You look pretty good, too. You clean up real nice—out of your sweaty T-shirt and gym shorts."

They had met at the health club and after two months of talking on neighboring treadmills, Joel had finally found the courage to ask her to dinner. Clear evidence that he was terrible at dating, he'd invited her to a continuing-education symposium. He'd considered calling to change plans but didn't want to complicate things or give her any reason to cancel. So here he found himself, meeting his first date in many years at the Drake Hotel to listen to a bunch of physicians talk about a surgical cure for obesity.

Even if the venue was wrong, the effort represented progress. Tonight was an attempt to steer his life in a different direction. Since confessing his long-held secret to his father about the role he had played in his brother's death, Joel had found a freedom that had for years been missing from his life. He decided to correct the trajectory of his downward spiral by ending his self-imposed penance and allowing himself to enjoy the company of a woman, something he had inexplicably denied himself of for most of his adult life.

"Yeah," he said, straightening his tie. "Not bad for a guy who usually drips sweat on the treadmill next to you. Here." Joel handed her a nametag. "Sorry. Everyone wears one at these things."

She looked at the tag and squinted her eyes. "Yuck. No one ever calls me this—not even my father when he's angry with me."

"Abigail?"

"No. Never."

"No problem," Joel said, taking a sharpie and crossing out *Abigail*. He wrote *Abby* above it. "There. Much better."

"Well, now it looks messy."

"No one'll notice. Half the people inside will be asleep."

"It can't be that bad. What did you say the topic was?"

"Gastric bypass. Should be very interesting for you—a few long presentations filled with disgusting photos of wide-open abdomens and a bunch of medical jargon."

"Sounds fun," Abby said with a sour look.

Joel put his hand to his forehead. "I'm such an idiot. I

don't know what I was thinking asking you to this presentation. But don't worry. We'll have dinner first, and I doubt you'll make it to the slide presentation. These guys'll have you snoring in ten minutes."

"I'll drink coffee."

"You'll need more than coffee."

With a light hand on the small of her back, Joel led Abby into the large ballroom with a feeling deep in his gut that told him there was something special about her.

Chapter 20

Fishing

Friday, May 5
11:42 p.m.

Ben's eyes flickered in wild saccades as he slept. Lightning flashed and a jagged bolt of electricity ignited the clouds and brought the night sky to life. The crack of thunder was nearly instantaneous, and it shook the walls of the shack. He opened his eyes and took in his surroundings. Before he could orient himself, a fierce gust of wind broke the bolt that secured the door, whipping it open with such force that it crashed into the adjacent wall. Blue light from another lightning strike filled the shack before it was gone. Horizontal rain came through the doorframe.

Ben jumped from bed, put his shoulder to the door, and forced it shut. This was one of the worst storms he'd encountered on the island. He fortified the bolt and returned to bed. He closed his eyes and tried to sleep, but something had changed. His insides stirred with anxiety, and an overwhelming urge to be home filled his heart. He longed to lie in bed with his wife and hold her tight. But something was off tonight. The connection he had always felt to Abby, the link that had helped him survive this long into his journey, felt weaker somehow.

He closed his eyes and tried to sleep away the worry. But the booming claps of thunder prevented sleep from coming. Something was wrong. He could feel it.

The storm passed during the night, and Ben woke to blue skies. He sat in the chair outside his shack now, the wreckage of the airplane in front of him. Not even the passing of a year could allow him to get over its size. The nose had skidded across the ground until it came to rest at the edge of the lagoon, which swallowed the front portion of the plane, bringing the waterline to the middle of the cockpit windshield. Ben felt small and weak whenever he stood next to the wreckage.

The airplane's arrival in this spot had come with a destructive path of flattened trees and gouged earth where it had slid from the ocean and onto the island. The back half of the aircraft was missing, torn away during the crash and resting somewhere on the bottom of the Pacific Ocean. The plane had smoked for days after the crash, and Ben had taken shelter in the rain forest with William, watching and waiting for an explosion that never came. When the smoke stopped spiraling, Ben had finally climbed inside the wreckage to assess the damage and see what he could salvage. It had taken him a while to overcome the guilt of looting the random pieces of luggage he'd found. The only thing he wanted to find was missing, until William discovered it washed up on shore.

Ben pulled the journal from his backpack now and placed it on his lap as he sat in front of his shack. He opened the cover and thumbed to the passage he was looking for. He had been unable to shake the feeling that overwhelmed him during the night, the sense that something had happened with Abby.

He looked down at the journal and read, hoping the words would settle him.

The Summer I Learned to Fish

I learned to fish when I was eight. The aluminum boat was dented and dirty and rented from the old man at the marina every Saturday morning that summer. It was the year I learned from my father how to tie spoilers and hook shiners. It was the summer I learned how to thumb a casting rod and the nuances of jigging crawlers. It was when I learned how to tie my lures to the end of my fishing line.

"Over, under, and through the loop."

They were my dad's words, but I took them for myself, repeating them a thousand times that first summer as I mastered the Palomar knot I used to tie my rigs. I repeated the words at summer camp and while the family vacationed in the Grand Canyon. I repeated them at the dinner table and before I went to bed. In my dreams I tied the knots, oftentimes waking with the words on my lips.

"Over, under, and through the loop."

By the close of summer I had become proficient at tying my own lures, proud that I never needed assistance from my father—always mouthing the words as my fingers worked.

"Over, under, and through the loop."

That more than a month of Saturdays passed during that first summer without catching a fish was immaterial. I didn't have to catch the fish myself. I was satisfied helping my father land the largemouth bass that he hooked. I was happy retrieving the lures from their mouths and watching my father handle the fish. Many times, my father

*had offered his own pole when a fish was hooked
and the rod bent, but I had always refused.*

*"I want to catch my own, Dad. Without any
help."*

"Okay. Grab the net and help me boat this one."

*Netted and examined, the fish was released be-
fore we threw our lines back into the water. Then,
during a hazy July morning on Cedar Lake, it happened. A subtle flutter at the tip of my fishing rod.
Then a jerk.*

"I got one!"

My father smiled. "Okay, kiddo. Set the hook."

I yanked the pole skyward.

*"Perfect. Now reel it in. Keep tension on him,
no slack. Set your drag a little tighter." My father
grabbed the net. "Keep coming, keep coming. It's
a hog."*

"It is?"

*My father reached over the side of the boat and
swiped the fish from the water. It flopped in the
net. "Nice fish," my father said. "Six pounds,
easy."*

*I cautiously took the bass by the lower lip, like I
had seen my father do several times over the summer. I lifted the fish and slowly retrieved the Ra-
pala.*

*"Look over here, Ben." My father was staring
through the viewfinder of a camera.*

*I stood and held the bass high in the air. Years
later, my father and I would have many photos of
the two of us fishing together. My favorite is
framed and sitting on my mantel. In it, my dad and
I are in northern Canada, both of us holding huge
walleye that were caught simultaneously. The*

photo always reminds me of those Saturday morn-
ings, which became a part of my life that sat apart
from all the others.

"Dad," I said on the way home that day I
caught my first fish. "When I have a son, I'm
gonna teach him to fish just like you taught me."

My father smiled and reached over to tousle my
hair. "I hope your kid is as smart as mine," he said.

Had you been in my life more than our abbrevi-
ated time together, one of my great joys would
have been teaching you to fish and passing all your
grandfather's tricks on to you.

Ben looked up from the journal. The memories of his father, those Saturday mornings, and his wish to one day teach
his own son to fish had transported him to a different place
and time. Somewhere far from the island where he had spent
the last year. But as he turned his attention away from the
journal passage, his thoughts drifted back to Abby and the
nagging feeling that something had changed. That somehow
he was losing her. That things were spiraling out of control
and that his plan may not work.

It wasn't the first time since he'd found himself on the island that Ben realized his life before the crash had gotten
away from him. Jacob's death had sent him spiraling once before, and although he had righted the wild trajectory of his
days, he never quite recaptured his life. He'd always meant to
get it back, to take a turn someday that would lead him in a
different direction, back to the person he had once been. But
the years slipped by, and when he thought back over his life,
he realized the last stretch of it had been spent unhappily, the
discontented years accumulating silently, the way plaque col-
lects in an artery, silent and unnoticed until it is too late.

Ben thought back to the day Abby had brought up the idea

of another child. Their first attempt at assigning meaning to their suffering and to their son's death had come with the decision to donate Jacob's organs. Helping other sick children allowed Ben and Abby to find purpose in Jacob's life. That difficult decision had worked. It had quelled their anguish and answered unanswerable questions about life and death. But when the temporary high of using Jacob's death and their own suffering to help others faded, Ben and Abby found themselves lost and wondering.

It was only Abby's resilience, Ben remembered now, that saved them both. During a self-imposed intervention, Abby booked a monthlong getaway to Lake Tahoe. It was there that Ben fell in love with his wife again, and where they both finally emerged from the pain of losing their son.

The following year Abby brought up the idea of having another child.

"Have you thought about it?" Abby asked.

"Not really," Ben said.

"I have."

Ben paused before speaking. "I can't, Abby. I can't go through that again."

"We won't be going through it again. We will be recovering from it. We'll be assigning meaning to Jacob's death, because he will be inspiring us to have more children."

He shook his head. "It feels like we're trying to replace him."

"We'll never replace Jacob. Having another child doesn't mean we'll forget about him. It means we're trying to move on. It means we're trying to be happy."

Ben nodded and offered a weak attempt at a smile. "Maybe. Let's think about it. Let's at least sleep on it so I can get my head around the idea."

It wasn't an absolute refusal, but it was close enough. Abby knew it as much as Ben. Having another child was not in the cards.

Ben took a deep breath now as he sat in front of his shack and recalled all the shallow and selfish things he had done to try to fill the void left by Jacob's death. All the foolish things he did other than the right thing. It ate at him that he had left behind a secret that was sure to affect his wife in ways he never meant for it to do.

As he closed the journal, Ben made a decision. He promised himself that if he ever made it back to his wife, he'd find a way to fix things. He closed his eyes and during a silent prayer made the same promise to God—that despite all his mistakes, he'd find a way to make Abby happy.

Chapter 21

Kitesurfing

Monday, May 8
10:32 a.m.

Christian Malone's net worth was tied directly to his tech company's stock price, and much like the wind direction, the exact value fluctuated daily, but it was solidly in the billions. He'd made his first fortune in college when he wrote the code for, and developed the software to support, a program that allowed users to store documents remotely from a personal computer. The software backed up the data it stored and allowed users a worry-free place to stockpile files and data without fear of losing them to a computer crash. He sold the technology for eight figures and promptly dropped out of Princeton to start his own software business, which was now a publicly traded, Fortune 500 company with more than ten thousand employees. He was thirty-five.

A team of managers, executives, and board of directors ran the company now as Christian mostly watched from the sidelines, jumping in when a developer needed his brilliant mind for coding or other abstract, behind-the-scenes details.

But over the last few years Christian had developed other interests and investments that excited him. He was always chasing his next fortune, and with nearly unlimited capital, his curiosities varied widely. For the last year or two, he had been zeroed in on the high-end travel industry.

He stood in the conference room, the windows of which looked out over Silicon Valley, and aimed his laser pointer at the map that was displayed on the screen in front of him. He twirled the red dot of the laser around Hawaii and then steered the pointer down the map until he found the small island where he knew his next fortune waited. This morning, he was pitching his latest idea to a small group of investors.

"This," Christian said to his audience, "is Valhalla Island. Accessible only by floatplane, boat, or helicopter, this island is as remote as it gets. It's not big enough to sustain a landing strip, so flying directly to the island will not be possible. Instead, guests will fly to Tahiti and then have a couple of options. They can choose to be shuttled via helicopter from the airport in Tahiti directly to the island; or, they can choose to be taken by floatplane, which will take about forty minutes from Tahiti.

"The plans include a two-story resort with a maximum capacity of fifty guests. Despite the remote location, it will be a five-star complex with all the amenities. People will be traveling from around the world, and the journey will be long for many of them. So when they arrive, they will be placed in the lap of luxury and want for nothing."

"What are the logistics of building in this remote part of the world?" one of the potential investors asked.

"Difficult," Christian said. "I'm not going to make it sound easier than it is. All building materials have to come in by boat, either from the US or China. Some of the timber can come from Tahiti. As you all know, I started this project two

years ago, all on my own and with no outside money. I didn't
get very far. We managed to get some basic supplies to the island and to erect a few temporary living quarters, not much
more than sturdy shacks that were meant to house the construction crews while they built the resort."

"Then you ran into a storm," another investor said.

"Correct. After we put up the shacks and had shipped
some early supplies to the island, Hurricane Earl popped up
and spun its way toward our little oasis. The timing was bad.
None of the structures that were erected were secured when
the storm hit, and we lost everything. The crew evacuated the
day before Earl arrived on the island and most everything
else was destroyed. I toured the site a couple of weeks after
the storm and stopped all plans to build. Haven't been back
since. That was two years ago."

"You lost everything on the island, including your
money," another investor said.

Christian nodded. "Back then it was my pet project. I went
in blind, and I went in fast." He opened his palms. "Everyone here knows I can handle a small financial loss. I hope
you all know me well enough to also understand that I learn
from my mistakes. This time I'm going in with a better plan,
not so cavalier, and with a bit of perspective. My biggest ob-
stacle today is that all the people who tell me what I can and
cannot do with my money are politely telling me that I cannot go back to the project alone. I need some investors. So
here's my pitch."

On the screen behind him, the graphics from a satellite
image of the South Pacific and the tiny dot Christian had circled with his laser pointer zoomed in to the island. An aerial
view showed an artist's rendering of a beautiful resort set on
a white sand beach, and a luxurious pool surrounded by palm
trees. The overhead view scanned across the small island,

through the rain forest, and to the other side. Here, on the windward side, the ocean rolled onto shore in huge, curling waves, and the palm trees bent toward the interior of the island as strong winds battered them.

"A luxurious resort situated in one of the most exclusive locations in the world, accessible only by those with resources. Yes," Christian said, "we are marketing to the wealthy. We know only those with money will visit and, I believe, frequent our resort. But there are exclusive resorts in every corner of the world. What makes ours unique?"

Christian pointed to the screen.

"The westward side of the island represents the best location for kitesurfing in the world. You all know I've been kitesurfing my entire life. It's like a drug. I've searched the globe for the best winds and the best waves, and I've never come across any better than what this island offers. The rich will come for the exclusivity of our resort, but they'll come *back* for the kitesurfing."

On the screen, a professionally shot video featured Christian and his friends kitesurfing off the westward shore of the island. The footage came from GoPro cameras mounted on the kite boards as well as overhead shots taken from drones. No expense had been spared in producing the video because Christian knew that the kitesurfing was the key to his pitch. Christian Malone had filled his office not just with those wealthy enough to invest in his resort, but those who also loved the sport.

When the video ended, the questions from his potential investors came rapid-fire.

"What sort of money are we looking at? And what kind of return?"

"What's your timeline?"

"We'd obviously have to test-drive the kitesurfing ourselves. When is the first time we all could get out to the island?"

Christian smiled. They were interested, and he had them hooked. "Let's talk specifics. And most importantly, let's work out a time when we can all take the journey to this little island so I can show you how mind-blowing the kitesurfing is."

NOVEMBER

Chapter 22

Harnessing the Wind

Wednesday, November 1
3:21 p.m.

Abby found her bench near Belmont Harbor. The breath of Lake Michigan was turning cold again and reminded Abby of her original visit here, when she braved the frozen temperatures after her lunch date with Maggie to sit on her bench and find a way through the previous Christmas, her first without her husband. Since Ben's death, the bench at Belmont Harbor had become her sanctuary, a confidant she visited often to vent frustration or work through emotions. The icy temperatures from the previous December had first been replaced by the thaw of spring, which then morphed to the warm exhale of summer. And now, as October came to a close and November began, the cool chill of fall.

All summer long she had watched the white triangles of sailboats fill the lake as she sat on her bench contemplating life and plotting the best route forward. During the summer, those sailboats had always been pitched at different angles and keels, all heading on scattered courses across Lake Michigan. But despite their paths, each sail fed off the same source—the same wind that blew from only one direction.

Abby had come to her bench and watched the sailboats throughout the week, when she needed a break from the day. She watched them all summer until the end of September, when the temperature dropped and the boats disappeared, pulled from the water and stashed for the season. Now, with Halloween and the end of October, the trees along the lakefront had taken on a glow of pumpkin and gold, the curbs and gutters heavy with fallen leaves that stirred with the wind and rustled as they somersaulted.

Abby reached into her jacket pocket and pulled out a red envelope. She looked at the return address again—*Joel Keaton*. It had arrived in the mail yesterday, but she'd waited until now to open it, until she was on her bench where she did her best thinking.

Boo! I was just thinking of you, the jack-o'-lantern card read. *Happy Halloween.*

The card was signed:

> *Let's get together soon. I miss our talks.*
> *—Joel*

A smile found her lips, although it was a nervous one. It had been a year and a half now. Almost eighteen months since she'd lost him. On some fronts, her world was back to normal. But on others, she was stuck in a hard-to-understand place of wanting but being unable to move forward. Her biggest step had come when she finally packed away Ben's belongings—starting the night she hid in her closet the constant memory of her husband that came with his watch and wallet resting on the dresser. In the days and weeks that followed, Abby took larger steps, storing his clothes and shoes. His ties and suits. His ball caps. She donated his golf clubs to the church fundraiser and sold his car back to the dealership. She tossed the architectural journals that cluttered the den and finally found the courage to enter his studio, where she disassembled the model of the building he had been designing, returning it to the partners at his firm. The hardest step by far, though, the trickiest of all and the one she took with the least sense of balance, came when she cleared the pictures that decorated her home: wedding pictures in the foyer and framed photos that hung on the walls all went into storage.

She kept only one: the photo of Ben and his father on a Canadian fishing trip holding fish in their outstretched arms, smiles that were larger than life. Ben was only twenty when the photo was taken, a few months before his father passed. The picture gave her a sense of comfort and, though she knew all the others needed to go, she kept this one on the living room mantel and looked at it often. It was a moment in time when Ben looked the happiest, before Jacob's death had changed him in ways he never recovered from. Abby tried to remember just the good times as she let go of the only man she had ever loved.

Her next step toward moving on was joining a gym. She had exercised little in the year after Ben's death, and although it hadn't shown on the exterior, mostly because she hadn't eaten either, she felt it inside. An unfamiliar fatigue that plagued the end of her days. The gym became her escape. A place to unwind and get away from the humdrum of repetition that had settled into her life. Work and home. Work and home. It went that way for more than a year until she met Joel Keaton. He changed everything.

She read the card again.

I miss our talks.
  —Joel

It had been six months since Abby had accompanied Joel to dinner at the Drake Hotel. It was her first date in over fifteen years, and the night had set loose an avalanche of emotions reminiscent of years ago. Feelings of excitement and anticipation and all the emotions that come with the unknowns of a new relationship. When the time had come that night to leave her house to meet Joel, Abby had made a decision. As she stood in the foyer making last-minute adjustments to her hair and makeup, her wedding ring caught a ray of light. She held her left hand in front of her and stared at the ring. Blocking the colliding thoughts in her mind, Abby cracked her wedding ring from the indent in her finger and placed it on the foyer table. Then, with a deep breath, she left the house to meet Joel Keaton for dinner.

In the months since that first date, they had shared coffee a few times, seeing each other mostly at the gym. Joel had asked her to dinner a few times since their night together at the Drake Hotel, but Abby always found reasons to refuse, none having to do with a lack of interest. He was good-looking and a gentleman, polite and courteous. He had a great sense of humor and Abby laughed often when they were together. Conversations came easily with him, and Abby realized she, too, missed their talks. But there was something else there. Something that kept her from opening up. Something she couldn't understand or identify. A sensation of uneasiness that had spawned during that first date with Joel. Perhaps, she told herself for the hundredth time, it was still too early.

She was glad for their time at the gym; it kept them in touch and gave them an easy place to see each other during the week. And it kept alive those feelings of possibility. Those feelings of anticipation that formed like bubbles on the bottom of an about-to-boil pot of water. The hope of seeing Joel at the gym gave her something to look forward to, and looking forward to things was a forgotten skill since her husband had died.

She read the card again. *Boo! I was just thinking of you.*

A chilled breeze rolled across the lake. Abby wished she could find the energy to break free, to shake loose from the reins that were holding her back. To overcome the phenomenon that was pushing her away from a man who might bring her happiness. She looked to the lake and remembered the sailboats of summer, scattered on different courses yet all working from the same source. Harnessed correctly, she knew, the wind could sail a boat in any chosen direction. As she looked out at the lake now, Abby wondered if that same principle didn't apply to life.

Chapter 23

Forgiveness

Wednesday, November 1
7:32 p.m.

The popcorn stopped crackling in the microwave and Joel poured it into the large bowl that sat on his kitchen counter. He dusted the top with salt and retrieved two bottles of IBC Root Beer from the fridge. The Yankees and Giants were in the World Series, which had run itself to Game 7 and the first day of November. It fell on his sister Rachel's wedding anniversary, and Joel had offered to take his nephew for the night.

"Uncle Joel, it's about to start," Brian yelled from the living room.

"Coming." With a root beer in each hand, Joel picked up the bowl with his wrists and walked into the living room where Brian grabbed the bottles of IBC.

"Strike? That was so outside," Brian said. "I hate the Yankees! They win every year. The umps give them every call."

"Relax," Joel said. "The Cubs will be back next year."

"I doubt it," Brian said as he settled with his popcorn.

The tumor had been benign, nothing more than an abnormal cluster of harmless cells. Brian's nodes were clean, and further testing and imaging had been negative. He underwent a variety of blood tests each month and full-body PET scans to assure no other growths were forming. The tests would drop to quarterly before long, then biannually, and eventually fade out. *Lucky kid,* Joel thought every time he looked at his nephew. It wasn't the first bullet the kid had dodged in his young life, but it was still a wake-up call. A sharp slap to the face that demanded attention. Not for Brian—adolescents rarely realize their mortality, and Brian in particular had been through so much that the discovery of a benign tumor was less concerning to him than a bad call in the World Series. But for Joel, it had been a watershed moment. He had decided never to forget the look on Rachel's face when he told her what he'd found. Others had offered similar expressions of fear and dismay after he'd delivered equally bad news, but this time Joel Keaton paid attention. He felt his sister's pain and acknowledged her grief. He allowed that night to change him. Compassion, Joel realized, *could* be part of his career. That day ignited a passion to live life to the fullest, and to stop allowing his past sins to hold him back.

The death of his brother thirty years earlier had set Joel on a course of self-loathing and through years of self-inflicted misery. But discovering the tumor in Brian's gut during a routine appendectomy had been enough to shift his perspective. He decided it was time to forgive himself for the role he'd played in his brother's death, and to start living his life outside the dark shadow of guilt under which he had spent the past many years.

When Abby Gamble stumbled into his life, Joel realized she was the first person in many years who made him happy. He asked her to dinner two days after he operated on Brian, an all-out assault on life and the first steps he had taken in many years that were solely for himself. Medical school had been a quest to fulfill his dead brother's dream, and becoming a surgeon was an effort to win favor with his father. During residency, he had pushed away the only woman he had ever cared about because of a burning need to inflict the same suffering on himself that he believed he'd brought to his parents and his siblings—especially his oldest brother, Brandon, who had taken the brunt of his father's anger about their brother's drowning death. Joel's entire adult life had been a montage of appeasements and compromises. Abby was the first thing in two decades that felt like freedom.

Their date had been one of those perfect nights, smooth around every corner—no awkward conversations, no second guesses—just two people enjoying each other's company. They had snuck out of the conference at the Drake Hotel just after dinner and well before the presentation on gastric bypass had started, Abby laughing at Joel's blatant escape after a free meal, compliments of the Midwest Conference of General Surgeons. They took refuge in the lobby bar and talked for the rest of the night. Because of the fluidity of the evening and how much fun they both seemed to have, Joel was left wondering for the last few months about Abby's reluctance to see him again. Their first date had been in May. Now, the summer had come and gone, and he still hadn't come up with any answers.

Game 7 lasted three hours, during which Joel and Brian talked baseball and strategy and out-managed the managers. Brian explained how his school coach was teaching him to throw a curveball. Movement was way more important than velocity, Brian said. It was why the greats like Maddux and Glavine pitched late into their careers.

The Yankees won in the bottom of the ninth. Brian buried his face in his hands. "Every year!"

Joel smiled. "The Cubs," he said. "Remember? They'll be back next year."

"Sure they will, Uncle Joel."

Brian helped clear the dishes from the living room. They watched the post-game celebration for half an hour before Joel let out a yawn. "Well, kid, after I drop you off in the morning, I've got a full day at work. I'm going to bed."

"You work a lot."

"Yeah, I do. When you figure out what you want to do, pick an occupation with better hours."

"I'm gonna play in the majors."

"Perfect. You'll only work six months out of the year. The extra bedroom's all set for you. Towels are in the bathroom for the morning. Don't forget to take your meds or your mom will kill me, and she'll never let you stay over again."

"I won't forget. I'm gonna finish watching the Yankees celebrate."

"Not too late. You've got school in the morning." Joel headed for the stairs.

"Uncle Joel?" Brian asked when Joel was at the foot of the stairs.

"Yeah?"

"How come you don't have any kids?"

The question caught Joel by surprise. "Well . . . I'm not married."

"How come you're not married?"

Joel laughed. "I guess I haven't found the right woman."

"Maybe it's 'cause you work too much."

Joel cocked his head. "Maybe. Good night, Brian."

"Night, Uncle Joel."

Joel was halfway up the stairs when Brian yelled after him again.

"Hey, Uncle Joel."

"Yeah?"

"If you ever have kids, I think you'd be a good dad."

Joel smiled. "Thanks, buddy. Half hour, then get to bed."

Chapter 24

A Leap of Faith

Saturday, November 4
10:02 a.m.

It was intangible and invisible. Like a breath of oxygen reigniting a dwindling fire, Abby felt rejuvenated when she woke. There had been similar moments over the last year and a half, instances of healing when she felt better than she had in weeks past. Where the hurt was far off, and life felt normal again. But today was a particularly profound phenomenon— different from the others. The pain was gone, that was part of it, but so too was the hesitation that had been holding her back.

As she tossed the down comforter to the side, the chill of the house seeped into her. November had brought the frontier of winter and it was time to turn the heat on, maybe add a blanket to the bed. In the shower she allowed the hot water to raise her body temperature. She blew her hair, straightened it, and applied her makeup while a feeling of anticipation vibrated in her stomach.

She headed to her office, feeling the need to visit the place where she was most productive, a place where she always managed to get things done. She used the back door and climbed the stairs to the second floor. Stepping into her glass-walled office, she closed the door, nervously pacing in front of her desk. The floor-to-ceiling windows overlooked Michigan Avenue, which was packed with the usual chaos of shoppers, tourists, and traffic. She took a deep breath and finally sat at her desk, where she tackled some stale paperwork to get herself warmed up. She reviewed the monthly numbers, dove into the multilevel-marketing numbers, and made a few calls to her top salespeople. Finally, she wrote holiday bonus checks to her managers. When she finished, she picked up the phone, took a deep breath, and dialed. Five minutes later, after she'd hung up, she smiled. She knew the environment of her work would force her into action. It always had. Her company was her passion, her cubbyhole where she climbed during good and bad times in her life.

Her business had started as a small boutique where she showcased the all-natural cosmetics she made herself. Over the years it had grown into a juggernaut. Expanding to cities from coast to coast, and evolving from cosmetics to skin care, her business was bigger now than she had ever imagined it would be. And it showed no signs of slowing down. The internet had made her products available around the world, and interest in her patented formula of mineral-only beauty products was spreading overseas at a startling pace.

She left the quiet of her office and spent an hour on the floor. The two-story salon and cosmetics shop was crowded—the norm for a Saturday—and she spent time mingling with employees and customers, complimenting the ones who were receiving facials and offering advice to those looking to ward off the pallor their skin would undergo during the winter months. A classic '80s Springsteen song ended and transitioned into The Chicks's "Landslide." Abby hadn't worked the floor for some time; she was usually holed up in the design studio or in her office, working on the marketing side of things. But being out amongst her customers and within the environment of the salon she had carefully designed filled her with nostalgia.

At midmorning she had an urge to visit the warehouse. She met with the floor manager and got a long overdue review of the packaging and shipping process. She helped put together a few orders, and it reminded her of when she had first started, when her business was young, and when she had, on her hands and knees, boxed and packaged each order herself before loading them into her trunk to hand deliver. Now she looked around the warehouse to see forklifts crisscrossing and hissing as their hydraulics lifted crates and placed them on conveyer belts.

Although she loved the business she had built, she missed the excitement that came at the beginning. When she wasn't sure how things would turn out. When she wasn't sure if she would succeed. And now, fifteen years after she designed her first line and made her first delivery, she found that same sense of nervousness and excitement as she stood in the warehouse. This time, though, her emotions stemmed from a different venture on which she was about to embark—one that had nothing to do with her career or cosmetics or skin care. Her excitement today stemmed from a different beginning, again not sure how things would turn out or if she would succeed.

At noon she said her good-byes to the warehouse staff, finished the paperwork in her office, and left through the back door. She was nervous and embarrassed and hadn't acted like this since college. Except for the Halloween card she had read earlier in the week, she hadn't communicated with Joel in almost three weeks. Although the invitations had come at a steady clip after their first dinner date a few months back, a man can hear *no* only so many times before he gives up. She had said no to dinner on a number of occasions, no to a movie, no to breakfast, and no to a Cubs game. Most recently she had declined Joel's invitation to watch the World Series with him and his nephew. In retrospect, Abby could never explain her hesitation. She could never figure out why she kept saying *no* when all she really wanted was to say *yes*. She blamed the convoluted mess of her life over the last year and a half, always listening to the voice that whispered *You're not ready*. But when she woke this morning, the voice was silent.

She took Huron east from Michigan Avenue, toward the lake, and pulled into the parking lot at Northwestern Memorial Hospital. Inside, things were calm for a Saturday afternoon. The cafeteria was sparsely populated with doctors and nurses sitting quietly around tables, steaming Styrofoam cups in front of them. Visitors stood in line waiting to pay for their food, and a few patients on leave from their hospital beds sat with relatives and picked at stale donuts.

When she spotted Joel, she stopped and analyzed him. He sat with legs crossed, a newspaper open on the table in front of him as he scanned the headlines. He was wearing navy scrubs under a long pale-blue coat and, not for the first time, Abby realized how handsome he was. He had a strong jaw and chiseled creases around his mouth and eyes, which were a piercing ice blue. The splash of gray at his temples told a story of long clips of concentration, a feature Abby found strangely attractive. It was a foreign sensation she had stopped fighting. Sensing an attraction to another man had brought guilt at first; now it was something else. The guilt was still there, but somewhere further back, cast into shadows by excitement and fascination.

She walked to the table. "Hello, Dr. Keaton."

Joel looked up from his paper. "Hey, you made it," he said with a huge smile. "I was starting to think you stood me up."

"No, I got hung up at my office. Sorry I'm late."

"No problem. I was surprised to get your call this morning. Sorry I don't have time for lunch, but I'm stuck seeing patients this afternoon. I hope coffee's alright."

"Coffee's fine. I just figured we'd get together, since we haven't seen each other in a while."

"Yeah, for sure. I've been trying to get together for a while," Joel said. "How do you take your coffee?"

"One sugar."

Joel returned a minute later with two coffees. "This is the worst stuff in Chicago, just a warning."

He handed her the Styrofoam cup.

"So what's been going on?" he asked. "I haven't seen you at the gym lately."

"Yeah, I've been busy with work. Out of town a few days the last couple of weeks. I've got to get back into it, though. I feel it now when I don't work out."

"That's your body yelling at you. It's a good thing."

"I guess it is," Abby said.

Joel leaned onto the table to cut the distance between them. "I've missed talking to you, Abby."

Her heart skipped at the comment. "So have I."

"Where's your office? Just around the corner, right?"

"Michigan Avenue."

"Have you—" His pager beeped. Joel closed his eyes, his face in a sour pose, as if he'd just drunk curdled milk. He grabbed the pager from his waist and read the message. "Come on, guys," he whispered to himself. He looked back to Abby. "I'm sorry. They need me upstairs."

"Oh, that's okay." She waved at him and smiled as her cheeks began to burn with embarrassment. "I just wanted to say hi. It's no problem, really."

She started to stand.

"Listen, I'll be done this afternoon," Joel said with his

hands in an open-palm surrender. "I can do much better than this awful coffee, I promise. How about dinner tonight? Or drinks . . ." He paused, waiting for a response. "Anything?"

Abby nodded. "Dinner. That sounds fun."

"Okay." Joel nodded. "Dinner. That will work. I'll pick you up at seven?"

She nodded. "Seven."

He held up the pager. "I've gotta run. I'll call you later for directions."

Chapter 25

Best Friends

Saturday, November 4
1:47 p.m.

Twenty minutes after she left the hospital, Abby climbed the stairs of the three-flat and rang the bell. The wind rolled off the lake and it was apparent that winter had its eye on the city. Abby stood with her hands sunk deep in the pockets of her North Face parka, a thick scarf wrapped around her neck and hiding her face. In addition to the frigid chill, the breeze also brought the familiar whisper Abby thought she had shaken. *You're not ready.*

The banquet with Joel months ago had been a giant step in the healing process, but the event had been amongst a herd of others. Dinner tonight would be something else. Just the two of them. A candlelit table with shadows running over their faces. Intimate. It would be an actual date, and Abby realized it might not be what she was after. She'd forced herself into this situation, waking as she had with an eagerness to see Joel and make a move in the forward direction. Now that she had set things in motion, she found herself digging her heels into the ground to stop things. Her immediate thought was to cancel. She had actually decided on that minutes after she'd left the hospital, with her cheeks still burning with embarrassment. She had devised an ill-conceived plan to send a text message telling him something urgent had come up. She had even started typing out the text in her car but threw the phone back into her purse before sending it. Now she found herself in front of the flat with her face wrapped in a scarf and her thoughts running wild. It was here that Abby knew she would get the advice she needed. This was the one place she knew she had to come to make the night happen. She knew that if she made it to this doorstep, it would make backing out of dinner impossible.

Maggie answered the door. Abby watched the quick register of her sister's eyes. Maggie always possessed a sixth sense and the ability to read Abby without a single word spoken between them.

"Something's going on!" Maggie said with wide eyes. "Nothing bad, but something. What is it?"

Abby hesitated.

"Tell me!"

Abby took a deep breath. "I have a date tonight."

"What!" Maggie's body vibrated like a six-year-old hearing the ice-cream truck. "Get in here!" She grabbed Abby and pulled her into the house. "Who is he? What's he look like? How did you meet? Why haven't I heard about this guy?"

Fifteen minutes later they sat across from each other at the kitchen nook, oversized cups filled with frothy cappuccino in front of them. Abby had updated her sister on Dr. Joel Keaton, their original meeting at the gym, and their quasi-date months ago.

Maggie cocked her head to the side. "You went on a date and didn't tell me?"

Abby rolled her eyes. "It wasn't a date. It was a work dinner about *gastric bypass surgery* with about a hundred other people. We drove separately and went home the same way."

"Did you kiss him?" Maggie asked in a hurried, kid-like voice.

"Maggie!"

"Answer the question! Did you kiss the guy or not?"

"No."

A short pause.

"Did you sleep with him?"

"Jesus, Maggie! I just told you I didn't even kiss him."

"So? You don't have to kiss a guy to sleep with him." Maggie's voice took on a whispered, conspiratorial tone. "Back in college, before I met Jim . . ."

"Oh God. Don't. Please stop. Please don't tell me any more."

"Forget it." Maggie looked away. "Sorry. But in my state I need all the information I can get. I'm living my sex life vicariously through others."

Maggie had just entered her third trimester of pregnancy and was penguin-walking with her inflated belly.

"Jim's so freaked out about hurting the baby that we haven't had sex in two months. I don't think I'm going to make it. All my friends, exact opposite. Never *thought* about sex when they were pregnant. Me? I'm interested more than ever. Horny in ways you can't imagine. The sex dreams I'm having? They'd blow your mind."

"Please stop talking," Abby said.

"And I'm not the only one," Maggie said without pause. "This is not an unusual problem. I looked it up online. For a lot of women, libido *increases* during pregnancy." Maggie took a sip of her cappuccino. "And my husband has turned celibate. Lucky me."

"Okay, little sis. Too much information on *way* too many fronts."

Maggie nodded. "I'm done. Just explaining why I'm so desperate for information."

Abby lifted her cup. "How's the baby?"

"Good. Everything's on schedule. The baby is healthy and growing, and I can't believe I have to carry him for three more months. By New Year's I'm going to look like the Goodyear Blimp."

"Please. You're a stick figure with a potbelly. How's Jim doing?"

"Not good," Maggie stirred her cappuccino. *Decaffeinated,* she had pointed out to Abby to avoid the lecture from her older sister. "Besides his sex phobia, he fainted at birthing class the other day."

Abby laughed. "No he didn't."

"Yeah, he *did*! Had to be revived and everything. Paramedics, ambulance, the whole nine yards. It was so embarrassing. They propped him up after he came around and poured a can of orange juice down his throat, told him it happens all the time. Low blood sugar and vasovagal, and blah blah blah. But if he loses consciousness when he watches a stranger give birth during an educational video, what the *hell's* going to happen on the actual day of my delivery?"

Abby kept laughing.

"It's not funny. You're going to have to be in the delivery room with me. I can't go through it alone."

"I'll be there whenever you need me to be."

"You better, because I know I can't count on my husband to be coherent. And I'm not letting Mom anywhere near the delivery room. Can you imagine?" Maggie's voice took on the nagging voice of their mother. "You're not trying hard enough, Margaret. If you want something badly enough, you have to fight for it. Now push!"

Abby laughed, doubled over at the spot-on impression.

"Yeah," Maggie went on. "She doesn't come near me that day. Promise me."

"I promise. I'll keep her away."

They regrouped and calmed down.

"Okay," Maggie said. "You've avoided the topic long enough. Now let me hear it. If that was last spring, when you went to dinner with this guy, why haven't you been out with him since?"

"I don't know," Abby said, shaking her head. "We've had coffee a few times. And I see him at the gym a couple times a week."

Maggie rolled her eyes. "Boring and pointless. Why haven't you been out on a *date* with the guy?"

"I guess I'm nervous. I don't know."

Abby watched Maggie's eyes as they strayed to her left hand. She suddenly felt the absence of her wedding ring, which she hadn't worn for months now. Still, with Maggie's gaze clearly focused on her left ring finger, she felt naked without it.

Maggie's pregnancy had shifted the family's attention, which for the last year had been focused on Abby and what she was going through after Ben's death. But for the last few months everyone had been caught up in the anticipation of the new arrival. Abby was not only happy for her sister, but grateful for the distraction. Today, though, she needed some of that attention from her younger sister. She finally wiggled her fingers until Maggie looked up and made eye contact.

"I stopped wearing it a few months ago."

Maggie reached across the table and took Abby's hand. "Tell me to shut up if I go too far," Maggie said. "And don't start crying when I tell you this, because if *you* get upset, *I'll* get upset, and the doctor told me to avoid being upset."

They stared at each other for a long time.

"I love Ben," Maggie said. "I always will. He was perfect for you. He was your soul mate. But for reasons we'll proba-bly never understand, he's not here anymore. And since he's been gone, my sister's been gone, too. Sure, I see her all the time. But not the Abby I've always known. Not the fun-loving person who constantly smiles. Not the Abby who used to fill the room with energy. Some stranger has taken her place. Someone who's sad and lonely. I don't blame you, and I don't pretend to understand what you've been through. But I know this: I saw my sister standing on my front porch an hour ago. I saw her for the first time in more than a year. I saw that fun-loving, energetic person with a spark in her eye. She's been missing for a long time, and I was really happy to see her."

Maggie's eyes welled with tears.

"I miss that person. And I want her back in my life. I don't know this guy, Joel, from a stranger on the street, but it sounds like you like him. And I know you've already considered canceling tonight. I know you came here for advice. Maybe you came because you knew I'd never let you cancel this dinner date. Not in a million years." Maggie squeezed Abby's hand a little tighter. "Don't cancel, Abby. I haven't seen you like this in so long, and the thought of you going home to be by yourself tonight rather than to dinner with this guy makes me want to cry, and I warned you not to do that. It's okay to go out with another guy, Abby. He's not a replacement. Ben can never be replaced, but I know he'd want you to be happy. And this guy might make you happy. But if you cancel, you'll never know."

Abby took a deep breath, blinking away the tears that were forming. "I knew it."

"Knew what?"

"I knew my younger, immature sister would say something to get me back on track. Back to where I was this morning."

"Thanks." Maggie made an ugly face. "I'll take that as a compliment. So you're going on this date, right?"

Abby nodded. "I'm going."

Chapter 26

That Big

Saturday, November 4
7:12 p.m.

Abby showered, dressed and busied herself with enough preparation to suppress her nervousness. But when the doorbell rang, a wave of apprehension crashed over her and then quickly passed, like diving into an ice-cold pool and then walking the steps of the shallow end into the hot sunlight. She had decided to do this; her trip to Maggie's had made it impossible to back out. And now, with nowhere to go but forward, Abby chose to jump headlong into the unknown.

She wore a red dress that hung suspended just above the knee like a sea plant swaying in the current. Her auburn hair was flat-iron straight and her skin dusted with just enough makeup to highlight her high cheekbones and bronze her olive-toned skin. She took a deep breath and opened the door.

"Hi," Joel said. He was wearing a crisp Marc Jacobs sport coat and silk tie under a long trench coat. When he smiled the creases on his face moved in perfect unison, originating at the corners of his blue eyes and falling subtly to the edges of his lips. She took in his square jaw and broad shoulders and noticed that he had matted his graying temples close to his scalp in an effort to camouflage their presence. He looked even more handsome than she had considered that afternoon in the cafeteria. It reminded her of their first dinner together, which felt like a lifetime ago. "Come on in. Do we have time for a drink?"

"For sure," Joel said. "I'm actually on time for a change."

"Let me take your coat." She moved behind him and reached up to his collar. She felt the firmness of his arms as she pulled the trench coat off his shoulders. It unlocked emotions she had suppressed for months, and Abby felt her insides tighten.

She hung the coat in the closet. "How was your emergency?"

Joel shook his head. "Car accident. Ruptured spleen. Sorry again about that."

"For a ruptured spleen? I'll forgive you. Come on in. I've got beer, wine, scotch, and just about anything else you can think of."

"Wine would be great," Joel said as he followed her into the impressive home. "Your place is gorgeous."

"Thanks. I can't quite seem to settle too long on a single style, so it's constantly a work in progress."

Abby walked to the large built-in bar off the kitchen and poured two glasses of Silver Oak cabernet that had been stashed in the wine rack and untouched for more than a year. They sat at the kitchen table.

"I've never asked," Abby said. "Gastric bypass, ruptured spleens. What type of surgeon are you?"

"General. I do a little bit of everything. I've removed a bunion from an old man's foot, a young woman's thyroid gland, and just about everything in between. Family tradition. My grandfather was a doctor, my father, my oldest brother."

"Do you all practice together?"

"Practice medicine? No. My oldest brother, Brandon, is out in the suburbs, and my dad is . . . um, currently dying in hospice care." Joel shook his head. "Wow. That came out the wrong way. Sorry, I didn't mean to start the evening that way."

"No, not at all. Sorry to hear."

"Thanks."

"Is it . . . bad? I mean, obviously it's bad if he's in hospice. Is it . . . close?"

Joel nodded. "We all think so, but he's hung on longer than anyone predicted. I visit every day. I was there today, just before I came here. We're all just sort of waiting for it to happen. But there's a reason he hasn't let go yet, and I'm going to make sure I see him every day. Make sure he knows I'm with him until the end."

Abby smiled. "You're a good son."

Abby saw Joel's forehead wrinkle.

"I'm not sure that's true. At least, I haven't always been. But I'm trying now, and well . . . better late than never."

"Did you guys have a falling out?"

"Uh . . ." Joel's eyebrows rose as he wobbled his head back and forth. "No, not exactly. But, you know, we've had our ups and downs, and there're plenty of things I would change if I could go back in time."

"Sounds like most people's relationships with their parents."

"Probably."

Abby twirled her wineglass, looking for a way to change the subject.

"So tell me about your job. Do you like being a surgeon?"

Joel paused briefly before answering. "Let's just say I don't think I could do anything else. It's all I've ever known. I was just a kid when I realized I had to become a doctor."

"*Had* to? You mean because of your father?"

"That was part of it. There were other reasons, too. But that's a topic for another night. Do I love it? I don't know, it has its moments . . . and then there's the rest of the time."

He took a sip of wine.

"I'm just being pessimistic. It's all good. So how about you? You're in cosmetics?"

"I design them."

"For which company?"

"AG Cosmetics."

"That name rings a bell."

"Well," Abby said with a bit of reluctance, "it's a big company. We're pretty well known."

"Headquartered where?" Joel asked.

"Here in Chicago."

"Really? What's 'AG'?"

Abby smiled. "Abby Gamble."

"It's *your* company?"

"Yes. I started designing in college."

"And you own the company?"

"Yes, I started it right out of school."

"How'd you get into that?"

"It was a hobby. I started making my own lip gloss during my sophomore year of college, and all my friends told me I should sell it. When I entered a trade show, I sold out in the first hour of a three-day show. It inspired me. I guess I'm lucky, because at twenty I knew exactly what I wanted to do for the rest of my life. Lip gloss led to lipstick, which led to eyeliner, which led to toner, and on and on. Fifteen years later and I have lines of every major cosmetic. Plus moisturizers, skin care, and hair products."

"Really? I'm an ignorant male so don't get upset about this

question, but what's so great about your makeup versus everything else out there?"

"It's all natural, for one. It's a patented formula that in-
cludes no oils or chemicals. Only pure minerals. It's healthier
and keeps your skin younger—proven scientifically. We em-
ploy a leading dermatologist to oversee the clinical testing. We
even have a line of moisturizers specifically for cancer patients
who are undergoing radiation treatments. Almost entirely
eliminates the burning and destruction of the epidermis."

"Now I'm impressed."

"We actually have a complete medical side to the skin care
division. A cream to prevent stretch marks during pregnancy—one that actually works. Another to eliminate and
reduce scarring after surgery. A tetracycline-based lotion for
acne."

"And you created all these formulas?"

"I had a lot of help, and the clinical products were something that came later, after we brought in Elaine Corrington.
She's our resident dermatologist, the one who's in all our ad-
vertisements and commercials. But it was my idea to go more
natural and eliminate the chemicals and oils. There have been
a lot of copycats along the way, but we're definitely leading
the pack."

"Wow. And you started all this in college?"

"I *started* it in college. The lip gloss was made from
beeswax—sort of an accident in my Chem 101 lab. Things
grew from there. I wasn't this big back then, of course."

She could see the curiosity in his eyes.

"How big are you?" Joel asked.

Abby smiled. "Big."

"Give me an example."

She shrugged. "Two production plants, a dozen warehouses,
and a central distribution center."

"Damn. How many employees?"

"Total? Close to twelve hundred, not including the part-timers who do home shows and cosmetics parties and who make up the multilevel marketing side of things. If you count them, it's closer to four thousand."

"Good Lord. All for your Michigan Avenue location?"

"No. I'm in eighteen cities. New York, Boston, Miami, LA, San Francisco." Abby took a sip of wine and noticed the stun in Joel's eyes. "So," she said. "*That* big."

"How many partners?"

"Just me. Although I hired a chief operating officer five years ago to take some of the load off. She mostly runs things now with her team. I spend my time designing. It's my passion. And with someone else running the show, I was able to slow down a bit. I'm still a workaholic, don't get me wrong. But I've never been a nine-to-fiver, and since college I've always promised myself a little freedom. I take Fridays and Mondays off and hit it hard in the middle of the week."

Joel laughed. "I haven't had a four-day weekend in years."

"Years?"

"Put it this way: Since I started my own practice, I've never once taken a vacation. Almost seven years."

Abby shook her head. "That's not healthy, Dr. Keaton."

"Tell me about it."

"I had a mentor who helped me a lot when my company started to grow. She told me a business should be like a tree—it needs to be nurtured when it's first planted. It takes a lot of time and effort to make it grow. But if you stick with it and do it the right way, soon the tree grows on its own, and after a while it provides shade for you to relax under."

Joel pursed his lips. "I think I screwed something up when I planted my tree."

Abby laughed.

"How old is your company?"

"Fifteen years."

"So let's get this straight. You started your own company out of college; I went to medical school. You've got a mountain of employees; I have a mountain of debt. You have four-day weekends; I work *every* weekend. At least tell me with eighteen locations you have a grueling travel schedule."

Abby smiled. "I used to. I have people who travel for me now."

"Money's probably not that good." He cocked his head. "A lot of business debt, with a bunch of risk and worry?"

"Company's been debt free for three years." She kept smiling. "And I'm comfortable, without any financial anxiety."

"Difficult to manage all those employees? Lots of headaches and PR nightmares?"

"We're like a big happy family. Even take team-building trips to—"

"Okay, okay. I can't take any more. I look like a failure next to your resume."

"Hardly. No one's calling me to save someone with a ruptured spleen."

Joel shrugged. "That's lost its magic a bit, if there was ever any to begin with." He looked at his watch. "We'd better get going. Reservations are at eight. It's only a few blocks. We can walk."

They talked for six blocks. Just like the first time they had gone out, when they snuck out of the conference and talked for hours at the hotel bar, the conversation was neither labored nor boring. Abby sensed that Joel enjoyed hearing about her life, and for once she wasn't shy about sharing personal details about herself.

"You really have an amazing story. Your business, I mean," he said.

"Yeah, I guess," Abby said. "I put up a nice front, but the truth is that I'm still amazed at how things have grown. It sort of happens when you're not watching, you know? You get so caught up in the day-to-day that you don't see your progress until you stop and look back. I'm sure you know the feeling. You didn't get to where you are overnight. It took years to get through school and start your practice."

Joel nodded. "I never thought of it like that. Or maybe I've never looked back."

Abby had no idea about the many reasons for Joel not to look back, or about the carnage in the wake of his life that made looking back painful and moving forward difficult.

He pointed to the entrance of the restaurant. "It's right here."

They were seated at a small table, elegant and set for two, where their conversation slipped into dinner, both wondering why they hadn't done this since the previous spring.

"I thought I scared you off," Joel said after their entrées arrived.

"How's that?"

"The conference a few months ago. I thought I may have bored you to the point that you'd never have dinner with me again."

Abby shook her head. "No. It's just that . . . things have been busy at work. Trying to get the new line out and . . . other things in life."

"Yeah. Things have been a little crazy for me, too. But maybe I should have tried harder because I like being around you."

The tightness in her stomach was constant now, and Abby was surprised that she was enjoying the sensation, a feeling of anticipation she had lived without since Ben had died.

"So now that I'm feeling terribly inadequate because of your career success," Joel said. "I have to ask you another question."

"The way you say that makes me nervous."

"It's not that bad, just totally inappropriate. How old are you?

Abby squinted and smiled as she twirled the stem of her wineglass but didn't answer.

"Let's see, you started your business in college fifteen years ago, so that makes you . . ."

Abby let him do the math for a minute as she took a sip of wine. "Thirty-four. I turn thirty-five in February."

Joel exhaled. "Thank God."

"Thank God? What's that mean?"

"Well, you look *younger* than thirty-five. And I'm *older* than thirty-five, so I was worried there for a minute. But we're okay."

Abby crossed her arms and sat back. "Well, now I *have* to ask."

"How old I am? My birthday is on New Year's Day. I'll be forty."

"You're *forty* years old?" Abby said with wide eyes and feigned surprise.

"No, I'm thirty-nine. I still have two months until New Year's, and I'm going to enjoy every minute of it as a thirty-something-year-old."

"Your fortieth birthday on New Year's Day, huh? I'll have to remember that. A new year for the rest of us; a new decade for you."

"Thanks. I can't wait now."

"I'm kidding. Forty is nothing for guys. I hear the real midlife crisis comes at fifty."

"Fifty is too far off for me to worry about. Forty is what's got me concerned. I'll probably be completely gray by forty-one or -two."

Abby reached across the table and pinched a finger full of his graying temples. His hair was cropped short on the sides. "You could run a darkener through this and make it match the rest of your hair. I have a special blend at my store."

"Really?"

"You could, but I wouldn't." She sat back. "I like your hair. Graying temples mean you're distinguished."

"Maybe when you're sixty, or if you're an airline pilot. But on me, they just make me look old."

Abby shook her head. "A lot of women find graying temples sexy."

Joel raised his eyebrows. "Really?"

Abby shrugged. "Yeah . . . some do."

She was happy for the interruption when the waiter offered a dessert menu, which they each turned down. Outside they walked the sidewalk in a slow stroll back to her place. The six blocks still raced past. They crossed the street when they reached Abby's townhouse.

Joel walked her up the front steps, and they both stopped when they approached the door.

"I had a really nice time tonight," Abby said.

"Me too. Maybe we can do it again."

"I'd love to."

"So, let's say, next April?"

Abby laughed. "Maybe we shouldn't wait that long."

"Maybe not."

Joel leaned in and kissed her. His lips were full and soft and different in many ways from the only other man she had kissed in the last half of her life. The kiss was smooth and innocent, but with something more intimate just below the surface. As if all it might take was Joel's hand on her hip or hers on the back of his neck to turn it into something more.

Abby fought her first instinct to pull away, and then resisted her next to prolong the moment. In the end, she placed her palm to his cheek and allowed their lips to meet for a few more seconds, eyes closed and lost in the colliding sensations of joy and doubt. She slowly broke away, still with her hand on his cheek.

She was suddenly feeling awkward, with her eyes darting

from his lips to the ground. "Good night," was all she could think to say. It came out in a different tone than the rest of the evening, and Abby wished she could rewind and do it all again. Slower and with a clearer mind.

"Everything okay?" Joel asked.

"Yeah. It's just . . ." Abby smiled and nodded her head. "Good night."

She unlocked the door and stepped into her foyer. When she closed the door, she stood with her back flat against it, her heart drumming inside her chest and a strange feeling of guilt keeping pace with the beat.

Chapter 27

The Deer

Saturday, November 4
11:26 p.m.

Joel's condo was twelve blocks away. He made his way slowly along the sidewalk, ignoring vacant cabs and in no great hurry to get home. He wondered how she could have such a hold on him. How she could occupy such a piece of real estate in his mind despite barely knowing her. He'd been closed off from these feelings for so long and now, suddenly, they dominated his thoughts. His days changed when he saw her. She was on his mind every time he walked into the health club hoping to see her. And after he did, she stayed in his thoughts long after he left.

But he sensed that there was something holding her back. It could be that he was just bad at this sort of thing. The answer could be as simple as him being no good at reading and understanding women—his history of sabotaging his previous relationships was certainly a testament to such an argument. Or it could be that Abby was not interested. The way she had pulled away on the front porch a few minutes earlier certainly suggested a hint of indifference. But because the rest of the night had gone so smoothly, the scene on her front porch had left him puzzled. By the time he reached his condo, he was fatigued. Abby Gamble was a mystery. One he was not sure he would be able to solve.

He'd be forty in a couple of months and playing games had never been his style. It took nearly an entire baseball season to get her to dinner again. It wasn't supposed to be this difficult—when it was, it usually didn't get much easier. But there was something too alluring about this woman to give up. He remembered how she had talked about looking back and seeing life's progress. The thought was intriguing now—getting lost in the moment with Abby and someday looking back to see their journey and follow the footprints they'd left behind.

When Joel's head hit the pillow an hour later it was filled with doubt, and heavy with speculation. A quiet voice whispered from the recesses of his mind that he didn't deserve her. That she was meant for someone more special than him, someone with a clean conscience and a healthy soul. He closed his eyes and fell asleep.

Joel found himself in his childhood home, a place he visited often in his dreams. He had asked his shrink friend the meaning one day over lunch and his friend responded that the house and the neighborhood in which he grew up were so deeply engraved in his psyche and had encompassed such a large volume of his life—nearly twenty years—that it was normal for the subconscious to return there during times of heavy slumber.

He was there now, wandering through his childhood home and remembering the large bay window in his father's study. Through it he was able to watch chipmunks and raccoons as they scurried through the forest against which the house nestled. He and his sister, Rachel, would watch for hours, kneeling on the couch in front of the window, elbows on the back-rest and chins on their hands. After some time, raccoons and chipmunks no longer satisfied them. The real game was spotting a deer, which they did from time to time. They'd often stare through the window for an entire afternoon, until the sun faded, and the forest grew dark.

Joel gazed now while he dreamt. It was sunny in his dream, and shadows laced the woods. He'd had this dream many times before and could nearly predict how it would play out—a deer would appear in the yard, just beyond the glass and so close Joel could reach through the window and pet it. But in this recurrent dream Joel ran from the window in search of his brother, not wanting him to miss seeing the deer. His search always led to the river. Depending on how his day had gone and the thoughts that cluttered his mind, sometimes Joel was able to convince his brother not to venture out over the fallen logs; other times he went along and watched again as his brother fell into the raging river. Occasionally Brandon was there in the dream to save them from the water. Other times Rachel was with them at the river, and together they would all decide to skip the crossing in lieu of racing through Gentry Cemetery and back home before dinner.

No matter which form the dream took, though, Joel always ended up with his brother on the couch, staring through the bay window. But when they finally got back to the couch in the den, the deer was always gone. Joel had never mentioned this portion of the dream to his psychiatrist friend—missed opportunities and failed commitments were how it would have been interpreted. Guilt and empty redemption were the truth.

Joel peered through the window now, almost knowing he was dreaming but not quite. He squinted harder through the glass, looking for the elusive deer. Instead, he saw a man step from the foliage, stare at Joel from the edge of the forest, and raise his hand in an amicable wave. Joel did not recognize the man, yet the sight of a stranger in his backyard produced no feelings of fear or trepidation. Joel slowly climbed off the couch and headed outside.

"Have you seen any deer lately?" the stranger asked as Joel walked into the yard.

Joel approached the man slowly.

"No. But there's one that comes out from the forest from time to time," he said. "I know it's the same deer because her eyes are like marbles, giant globes with caramel burned into them. And she's got a scar on her side, like maybe a hunter's bow had hit her once, but she managed to survive. I feel like she's close by, but too frightened to come out of the forest."

"Don't stop looking for her," the man said. "She'll come around again."

"I think she's scared. Like maybe I might hurt her. I never would, but I think that's what she's scared of."

"You've never hurt anyone."

Joel shook his head. His thoughts were congested suddenly with fear and confusion.

"It's okay to be happy, Joel."

"I could have saved him. If I had just told my dad or Brandon. I could've saved him."

Joel had a sudden urge to run to the river and find his brother. An ache deep in his heart made him long for the opportunity to talk his brother out of crossing the river that day. How different things would be had they decided to walk home rather than venture out onto that log. He and his brother had been best friends, even though Joel was six years younger. The age gap was large enough for Joel to have a mentor, but not so great that they couldn't have fun together. Their adventures at the river were just a small part of their bond, and Joel always wondered what sort of friends they might have grown into as adults. Theirs was a much different relationship than the one Joel shared with Brandon. Ten years separated Joel and Brandon, and the gap was too great to bridge in any meaningful way during adolescence, and since their brother's death at the river, the gap had grown wider.

The man pointed to the big bay window of Joel's childhood house. "If you keep looking through that window, your past will torture you forever."

The man turned and headed back into the thick foliage of the forest. Joel watched him leave and then looked back to the window of his father's den—the window of his childhood. The glass of the bay window mirrored the woods behind him, and Joel saw himself in the reflection. Not the ten-year-old boy he imagined himself to be in the dream, but the adult he was.

He woke without a startle or a jerk. He simply opened his eyes. The red glow of the alarm clock told him it was two-thirty in the morning. He drank a glass of water and tried to push the dream from his mind, but all he could think about was his brother being pulled away by the river. An hour later, when it was clear that he wouldn't be able to get back to sleep, he dressed in jeans and a T-shirt, walked out the front door, and headed toward the hospice facility. If he wasn't going to sleep in the middle of the night, he may as well spend the time with his father.

Chapter 28

Hanging Around

Sunday, November 5
9:22 a.m.

Abby and Maggie sat in the kitchen on cast-iron chairs and around a small glass table straight from the Pottery Barn catalogue, the same spot where Abby and Joel had shared a bottle of wine the night before. They sipped cappuccinos now. It was their drink, something they never shared with others. Somehow, sitting and drinking cappuccinos with a man made little sense. It was a drink for sisters and gossip, one that provided remedies for life's mysteries.

It had snowed overnight, the first snow of the season, and the sidewalks and street were covered in a blanket of white. The flakes continued to fall, filling the corners of the window frames. Maggie had called at promptly seven o'clock that morning.

"Are you by yourself?" she had whispered when Abby answered the phone. It aroused the desired response from her older sister—a stern denial—and Maggie was over a half hour later; Abby already had cappuccinos steaming on the table.

"Sort of?" Maggie said now. "What does that mean?"

"I don't know. It was a good-night kiss," Abby said. "A little peck."

"Mm-hmm," Maggie said, stirring her cappuccino but with her gaze fixed on Abby. "Lips or cheek?"

"Maggie," Abby said in an annoyed voice. "You're so obnoxious."

"Lips or cheek, dammit! Don't get a pregnant woman upset."

Abby rolled her eyes. "Lips."

Maggie sucked in a large volume of air. "Abigail! You little slut." She paused for a second. "Tongue?"

"Boy, are you desperate."

"Worse than desperate, I'm deprived. Jim won't even consider sex. He starts sweating when I get interested. He literally jumped out of bed the other night. I'm not exaggerating. Jumped out of bed and *ran* out of the bedroom when I asked if he wanted to have sex. Is my body that disgusting?"

"You're beautiful. He's just worried about the baby."

"Yeah, well, I gave him a crash course on female anatomy, explaining that the baby is more than ten inches from the exterior of my body, and I assured him he wouldn't come *close* to hurting the baby."

"I'm sure that conversation helped things."

"Not so much." Maggie shook her head. "I'm bitchy and horny, and my husband won't touch me. So, that's the latest on my pregnancy, in case you were wondering."

Abby forced a smile and raised her eyebrows. "I don't really want to hear about your sex life."

"*Lack* of sex life." Maggie waved her off. "Fine, I'll move on. So is this guy a good kisser?"

"It was a *peck*. And the whole thing was awkward. Not dinner, that was fun. But as soon as we walked up the steps to my door, things got all mixed up."

"Why?"

Abby exhaled a long, reflective breath. "I don't know. I'm an idiot."

"Do you like the guy or not?" Maggie asked.

"I *do* like him. A lot. So much that I think we might be right for each other. But it's all so confusing. My head and heart are pulling me in opposite directions."

"I don't get it. You either like this guy or you don't. You either want to kiss the guy or you don't. What am I missing?"

"It's like this," Abby said, her hands around the coffee mug. She was in her pajamas with her knees tucked to her chest and her feet on the chair. "When we were kids, remember when all you wanted to do was hang out with me and my friends?"

Maggie shrugged. "I guess, sure."

"You may have been too young to realize it, but my friends and I . . . well," Abby searched for words.

"Well, what?"

"Well, we hated hanging out with you."

"*What?*"

"You don't have a younger sister, so you'll never understand. But when you're a kid, an older kid, the last thing you want is your younger sister barging in on you and your friends."

"Excuse me for wanting to hang out with you when we were, like, *ten*."

"Maggie, I'm trying to make a point here. So when we were kids, when my friends and I were just about ready to do something fourteen-year-olds do, you'd show up and hold us up."

"What were you doing? You were *fourteen*. Shit, Abby, I was dating boys before you. *I* was helping *you* figure out how to get invited to dances. You wanted me around then, I remember. But I guess when your friends were around—"

"Maggie! It was twenty years ago. You're my best friend

now. Listen to me. When we were kids, you showed up at all the wrong times and now, well . . . Ben is doing the same thing."

Maggie slowly sat upright. "Oh."

"Exactly. Like last night. Joel and I were having a great time, conversation was easy. No silent gaps or awkward glances. No forced laughing or feigned interest or any of the stuff terrible dates are made of. Things are just easy with him. He was charming. He looked good. Really good."

This caused Maggie to raise an eyebrow.

"Then he walked me home and things went to hell. The whole time we walked, just the two of us, we passed other couples. They were holding hands and laughing. That's when Ben showed up. Planted in my brain like a perennial, blooming every time the weather gets warm. And God, Maggie, when we got to my doorstep I must have looked like a fool. I could barely look him in the eye because I was feeling guilty. When he spoke, I heard Ben. And when he kissed me, I went frigid." Abby bit her bottom lip and looked off. "He probably thinks I'm a thirty-four-year-old virgin."

Maggie snorted on her cappuccino. "We both know that ain't true. The back of a Honda Civic cured that ailment long ago."

"Come on, Maggie! I need your help."

Maggie grabbed Abby's hand. "Look, I'm sure he understands. You've told him, haven't you?"

"Are you insane?"

"You *haven't* told him?"

"That's just what every single guy's looking for. A thirty-four-year-old widow. Better yet, a widow who lost her husband a year and a half ago and is still, obviously, an emotional wreck. And one who has never really dated anyone else. Fifteen years, not one date. The only thing worse would be if Ben and I had been high school sweethearts. 'So along with me, Joel, you also get more baggage than any relationship can carry.'"

Maggie grabbed the tall, silver Thermos from the counter and refilled their mugs, then sprinkled nutmeg over the tops. "Number one, you don't have baggage. You lost your husband, and from what I can tell, you're doing pretty damn well. Shit, Abby, look at this place. Your house used to be a shrine of you and Ben. Pictures all *over* the goddamn place! You've put those pictures away, and I know that had to be hard for you. I was in your closet the other day—I know, I'm nosey, I admit it—and all of Ben's clothes are gone. Along with his watch and wallet, which hung out on your dresser for damn near a *year*!"

Abby crinkled half her face as though she smelled a foul odor. "Why were you in my closet?"

"I've noticed it all, Abby," Maggie said, ignoring her sister. "Including the day you stopped wearing your wedding ring. Yep," Maggie nodded her head, "noticed that, too, long before the other day when you thought you were showing me for the first time. So what I see is not a woman who's carrying around baggage. You're not an eighty-year-old who just lost her husband and wants nothing more than to spend the rest of her days in mourning 'waiting for the Lord to take her,' as Nana used to say. You're a thirty-four-year-old vibrant, independent, successful woman who wants to start living life again. And your life is going to include Ben; it has to. And it should. But it shouldn't *only* include Ben. It should include Mom and Dad. It should include me and Jim and your nephew, whenever he arrives. It should include your friends. And yes, Abby Gamble, a single, thirty-something woman's life should include a man or a boyfriend or whatever you want to call it. So let it. Let your life include all those things, and soon, I'll bet, just like me when I was growing up and earning friends of my own, Ben will show up less and less.

He'll always be there, Abby. In your memories, and in your heart, and whenever you think of him. But it doesn't have to be a bad thing. It doesn't have to be something that holds you back."

Abby blinked away tears and smiled. "See, this is why you're my best friend."

Chapter 29

The Way Back

Sunday, November 5
2:25 p.m.

There had originally been six shacks on the island. Three were still standing. The others were splintered piles of timber that had succumbed to a past storm. He was glad to have missed that storm. During his time on the island he had endured a few heavy downpours that lasted a couple of days and brought some fierce winds, but his meager shack had been sturdy enough to keep him dry and warm.

When Ben first arrived he had inspected the three remaining structures to determine their stability, discovering that each shack was constructed from six posts sunk deep into the ground, providing a sturdy base. The walls were made from tongue-and-groove wood, which kept out the strong ocean winds. Inside each shack he had found a thick mattress and box spring. The existence of the shacks represented much more to Ben than salvation. They gave him hope. They told him that however forsaken this island was, someone, at some time, had been here before. Maybe he had a chance. Maybe William and his father had a chance, too. But Ben had first found the shacks quite some time ago, and he feared that if he didn't make progress toward getting home soon, it would be too late.

He sat in his usual spot outside his shack and opened his journal. He had started writing letters to his son ten years ago. Originally they were a way to begin the healing process, but the letters eventually became something more. They became a link to his son, and he had never stopped writing them.

Ben turned the page and read the heading:

The Day It Happened

We placed you on a list to be considered for a clinical trial for an experimental drug. You had failed to respond to chemotherapy, as was predicted, and the chance that you might not live long enough to see the clinical trial was too torturous to consider. We placed your name on the list with hundreds of others and knew the odds were slim that you'd be selected. Not even the hope of some new, magical drug could change the inevitable. Your mother and I did it to feel like we were doing something. To make it feel like we weren't just sitting around waiting for you to die.

We were able to hold you for short spans. The rest of the time was spent by your side, listening to the whish-woo of the respirator, too scared to sleep for fear that the moment we drifted off would be the moment it happened, and if we woke to find you still with us it would have been time we had wasted away from you. Mostly we watched you sleep. We watched your chest rise and fall under orders from the respirator. Your mom was still praying for a miracle, I was too far gone.

You made it three months, overachieving what the

doctors thought possible. Strangely for me it was more torturous than if God had taken you on the day you were born, because during those months a bond formed between us, one that would forever weigh me down—like an anchor chained to the leg of a man adrift at sea, constantly tugging as he fought the water that rose above his head.

During those months in the neonatal unit, I whispered to you all the things we would do together when you were healthy. The baseball games I told you about served as temporary relief from the reality of our situation. The Saturday mornings I promised—where we would set out on the lake to hunt for bass, and where I would pass down to you all the secrets my father had taught me—were nothing more than my escape. The things I told you about were tiny havens where I found relief from the torment of watching you struggle. And as I write this letter years later, I can still close my eyes and see your tiny hand wrapped around my index finger. It was a much greater symbol than you holding on; to me, it was a son's plea for his father's help. I know that's irrational, but I was told to be truthful in these letters. I hope someday the feeling of having failed you passes.

Abby and I were on a thirty-six-hour stretch without sleep. We knew the end was near, and we both refused to give in to fatigue. We both insisted that we be with you and alert when you passed from this life to the next. Your mom held you in her arms while I held both of you. Your breathing had been labored and congested for hours, as the doctors warned would happen. Your skin was an absent gray, and your eyes hadn't opened in days. Abby cried inconsolably while she stared at you.

I stared too, guilty and ashamed of my helplessness.

Fathers are meant to protect their children, to shelter them from the cruelties that hide in the shadows, and to save them when their children cannot save themselves. But I was powerless as I watched your chest fall for the last time. I felt small and feeble as you lay silent and still in your mother's arms.

Ben looked up from the journal and stared at the ocean. He took a deep breath and wiped the tears from his cheeks. His heart ached for his son, but also for Abby. Remembering her sorrow while she held Jacob that day was too much to bear. Ben wondered what she was going through now. He tormented himself with thoughts of how alone Abby must feel.

As he moved his gaze to the torn wreckage of the airplane, Ben Gamble was filled with a sudden urgency. It was time to find his way back to his wife.

Chapter 30

Frozen Kitten

Friday, November 10
5:22 p.m.

The first ten days of November were wrapped in the type of cold for which the Midwest was famous. A nasty patch of frigid air had swept down from Canada and quickly turned the middle of the country into a frozen tundra. Snow followed. In just the first week of November, twenty-two inches had already fallen—a record for Chicago—and the run-up to Thanksgiving was promising to be brutal. Chicago was digging in for a bitter winter.

Lake Michigan whistled forty-mile-per-hour gusts off its surface that knocked pedestrians sideways and stopped them in their tracks. Abby was bundled unrecognizably as she walked, with her hood up and scarf wrapped high on her neck. She was coming from her bench at Belmont Harbor, where she had stopped after work to stare out at the lake and contemplate her life. As she walked down the sidewalk now, a teenager from the neighborhood shoveled the stairs of her townhouse; several porches along her street were already cleared of the afternoon snow.

"Evening, Mrs. Gamble," the kid said, pinching the brim of his hat like it was 1952.

"Hi, Lenny."

"Lots of snow today. Had to hire two friends to keep up. I invested in a snow blower because this is supposed to be a real nasty winter. Hear it?"

From down the block, the engine whined as it barreled through the snow. Abby nodded and smiled as she stood on her freshly cleared steps. "Good luck."

"Supposed to snow overnight. Probably be back early in the morning, so sorry if I wake you."

"That's quite all right, Lenny. Make sure to leave an invoice in the mailbox."

"Yes ma'am," Lenny said before getting back to work.

A car door slammed across the street and Abby saw a woman standing next to a parked car. She was bundled in a heavy coat and held a white envelope in her hand. The woman walked across the street to the curb in front of Abby's townhouse and stepped over a mound of snow to reach the sidewalk.

"Hi," Abby said. "Can I help you?"

The woman nodded. Her face carried a confused look.

"You're Abby Gamble, right?"

Abby paused a moment, pulled her hood down. "Yes. Can I help you with something?"

Abby noticed the woman was shaking. Possibly from the cold, but Abby thought it was something else. The envelope in her right hand trembled in the breeze.

The woman looked up to Abby's front door and at the address above the frame. She shook her head. "I'm sorry," she said suddenly. "I've got the wrong address."

The woman hustled back over the snow mound and started across the street. A car skidded to a stop and blew its horn in a long, angry blast that startled the woman. The driver's side window came down.

"Trying to kill yourself, lady?"

The woman hurried to her car, climbed inside, and quickly drove away.

"Who was that?" Lenny asked.

Abby followed the car with her gaze as it pulled down the street, turned at the intersection, and disappeared.

"I'm not sure."

Lenny went back to his shoveling. "Supposed to get six inches overnight. It's gonna be a real mess."

She finally took her attention away from the road and looked at Lenny. "Thanks again for all your hard work."

She climbed the stairs and, once inside, closed the door behind her, peeling the layers of winter clothing from her body. As she walked into the kitchen, the scent of the dozen roses on the table took her mind off the strange encounter with the woman outside. The roses had been thin and pre-bloom when they arrived but now were fully blossomed and tiered. She smiled when she remembered opening the door to see the deliveryman standing with a bouquet.

I had a great time, the note read.

The fiasco on the front porch hadn't scared him away after all.

It was Friday and the forecast for the weekend was miserable—cold and snowy. Abby unwrapped a granola bar and stood at the kitchen hutch as she sorted through mail. Her phone rang and she dug in her purse until she found it.

"Hello?"

"Hi," Joel said.

"Hey. Thanks for the flowers, they're beautiful."

"I hope you like roses."

"What woman doesn't? Did you survive the snow this week?"

"It's awful. And we haven't even made it to Thanksgiving. But that's why I'm calling. Are you busy tonight?"

"Uh, no. What do you have in mind?"

"I'll pick you up in an hour. Dress warmly."

"Where are we going?"

"Hats, mittens, everything. I'll see you soon."

The call ended, and Abby couldn't stop herself from smiling.

An hour later Joel double-parked outside Abby's house and climbed the stairs. He was wearing a crewneck fleece and ski cap, looking as though he had just come from the slopes of Vail. When Abby answered the door she took a second to examine him. The jeans and the boots and the cap covering his graying temples gave him a rugged appearance and an aura of handsomeness different from what Abby had noticed in the past. Something stirred inside her, the same as it had last weekend—an old sensation she had packed away some time ago but now was dusting off, like finding an old attic chest filled with childhood memories that transport you across time. She liked this place she found when it was just her and Joel. When she gave in to the sensation and allowed herself to enjoy it, Abby realized it was a place free from the congestion and confusion that had clouded her thoughts for the last many months. In this place, her grief was invisible. She loved that simply the sight of him brought her to this place and was frustrated that she wasn't strong enough to stay there. But she promised herself to try.

Joel smiled when the door opened. "You ready?"

"I think so," she said. "But since I don't know what you have planned, you tell me."

Abby held her arms out. She was wearing jeans that hugged her thin hips, and Columbia lace-up boots with a white Nautica ski jacket and pink gloves. When she pulled a hat onto her head, the ends of her auburn hair hung from the bottom and dusted the shell of her coat.

"Perfect. And you look cute, too," Joel said. "Let's go. There's someone I want you to meet."

He helped Abby navigate the mound of snow at the curb. He opened the door of his Range Rover and she climbed in. A young boy's head popped over the back of her seat.

"I'm Brian. Uncle Joel's nephew."

"Hey, Brian. I'm Abby."

"Have you ever been to the slides before?"

"The slides?"

Joel opened the driver's-side door and climbed in. "It was supposed to be a surprise, knucklehead." He looked at Abby. "I guess you've met my nephew."

Abby smiled and winked at Brian. "I figured we were doing something like that."

"Toboggan slides," Joel asked. "Ever been?"

"Never."

"Are you up for it?"

She smiled. "For sure."

"Yes!" Brian said from the back seat.

On the north side of the city, two fifty-foot slides sat within a forest preserve. The operators sprayed intermittent bursts of water from large hoses onto the slides, letting the frigid air freeze the water to a slick sheet of ice, which gave the toboggans a few extra miles per hour on the way down. Joel parked in the lot and rented two toboggans. Wooden with curled front ends, the sleds looked like elves' shoes. Red metal skis ran along their bottoms.

The park was packed with parents and children, teenagers and twenty-somethings, all bundled to the eyeballs. A battlefield was reserved for snowball fights. Kids screamed as snowballs sailed through the air and exploded on impact. Stadium-style lights brightened the open meadow and contrasted sharply with the black night beyond. Zigzagging staircases jetted up to the top of the slides. A steady pack of tobogganers shuffled the stairs, sleds in hand, waiting their turn. The slides sloped on forty-five-degree angles and after two hundred feet, spat their guests into a large opening covered with snow marred and streaked by sled skis.

"How fast do you go?" Abby asked in a hesitant voice as they started up the stairs toward the top of the slides, which suddenly looked more intimidating than they had from the parking lot.

"Like a hundred miles an hour!" Brian said. "It's so awesome!"

Joel shook his head slightly and leaned towards Abby. He whispered in her ear. "It's not that bad, or that fast."

She grabbed his arm. "You'd better not be lying. I get sick on roller coasters."

Joel slowly nodded his head. "Good to know. Maybe we ought to get you your own toboggan."

She threw her hip into him and as they climbed the stairs and kept a firm grip on his arm. A few minutes later they reached the top. Without hesitation, Brian plopped his sled into the grooved tracks of the slides.

"I'll go first!" He jumped onto the sled, his feet tucked under the curved front side and hands gripping the rope attached to it.

The operator, an elderly man who had been running the slides for three decades, asked in a cracked voice, "Are ya ready, son?"

"Ready!"

"Here we go," the old man said for the hundredth time that night. He grabbed hold of the crossbar above Brian's head and with his foot sent the toboggan into motion until gravity took over and sucked Brian down the long, narrow slide. A soft "whoosh" followed and grew in intensity until he was halfway down, when the sound disappeared into the open meadow. All that was left was Brian laughing and screaming.

Abby watched with terror as Brian picked up speed until

he reached the bottom, where the slide finally spewed him into the open field at what Abby estimated to be something greater than one hundred miles per hour.

"Ready, folks?" the old man asked.

"I'm, uh . . . I'm not sure. That looked a little faster than I expected," Abby said.

Joel placed the toboggan into the track. "You'll love it. Trust me. Come on, you get in front."

Abby put her mittened hand to her mouth as if she would bite through the wool to get to her fingers.

"All aboard, folks," the old man said. He had a schedule to keep.

"You heard him," Joel said, smiling.

She looked behind her to see a line of sledders waiting, their breaths steamy white as they exhaled into the freezing air. Abby felt their eyes on her. Snow fell silently around them, highlighted and glistening from the stadium-style lights. She turned back to Joel. "I'm scared to death," she whispered.

"I won't let anything happen to you."

"You better not let me fall out." She finally turned and climbed onto the front of the toboggan.

Joel sat behind her, locking his feet into the notches on the side so that his knees acted as arm rests for Abby. "I'll make sure you don't go anywhere." He reached around her waist and locked his hands near her navel, squeezing tight.

Abby reached back and grabbed the back of his head. "I'm scared to death."

"You already mentioned that," Joel said. "It'll be okay."

"Are you ready, folks?" the old man asked.

"Ready," Joel said.

Abby took a deep breath, pulled her hand from Joel's head and grabbed his legs as she held on for her life.

"Ready," she said.

"Here we go."

The old man footed them down the slide.

During the second when they hovered at the crest of the slide, before gravity tugged them downward, Abby realized this moment was the first time in nearly two years that she had been in the arms of a man. The first in over a decade that they were the arms of someone other than Ben. As the toboggan began its descent and her stomach shifted upwards, she leaned backwards into Joel. He responded by bear-hugging her and resting his chin on her shoulder. She closed her eyes and found comfort as he held her tight.

"Here we go!" Joel said. His lips touched her ear. "I've got you," he whispered. "I've got you."

As they raced down the slide, Abby barely realized they were moving. She was caught in his touch and in the way the coarse stubble of his face rubbed her cheek. The feeling took her to a different place—their place. She was starting to love it there. The feeling of it overwhelmed her sensation of falling, and the next thirty seconds were a blur. All she knew were his touch and his voice and his words.

I've got you. I've got you. I've got you.

"Wasn't that awesome, Abby?" Brian yelled.

When Abby opened her eyes, she saw that she was in the middle of the open field. Joel was laughing in her ear, still with his arms wrapped around her waist.

"What did you think?" he asked.

Abby looked back, amazed she had made it down the slide without realizing it, lost in Joel's arms, still grasping his legs and leaning backward into his chest.

"It was incredible," she said.

"Let's go again!" With his toboggan trailing behind, Brian ran toward the slides.

Joel unhooked his hands from her waist and rolled into the snow. He laughed harder. "I thought we were going to have to walk down all those stairs. You should have seen your face up there."

She scooped snow and threw it at him. "It looks higher when you're at the top."

He kept laughing. "You know they call it a 'frozen kitten,' when someone gets stuck at the top of the slides, too scared to go down."

"No."

"Yes. The old man gets on his radio and calls down to the ticket counter. Tells them he's got a 'frozen kitten on the Loft.' "

"Surprised they don't throw rocks at you, too."

"Worse. A kid from the booth comes up to escort you down the stairs. All the kids chant too, on the way down."

"Come on."

"Honest to God." Joel smiled. "Trust me. You were going down that slide one way or another. On the sled or over my shoulder, because Brian would never let up if we were the frozen kittens of the night." Joel started laughing again. "You must be a wreck at amusement parks."

She jumped on top of him. "Don't laugh. I was scared."

He nudged her off the sled so they were lying next to each other in the snow. "Even with me holding you?"

"No. That helped."

He leaned over and kissed her. The kiss lingered, neither in any hurry to end it. Joel finally leaned back.

"Wanna go again?"

"Sure."

"Brave woman."

After three more trips down the slide Abby and Joel took a breather while Brian barreled headlong up the stairs again, insatiable. A stand served coffee and hot chocolate. They cleared snow from a round picnic table where they sat and sipped their drinks.

"Do you watch your nephew a lot?"

"Yeah. But I don't think of it as babysitting. We're actually good friends. I know that sounds strange; he's only twelve."

"Not at all. I think it's cute. I can tell you guys are close. I bet it's important to him."

"Yeah. I'm his godfather, and we've always done things together, since he was little. Baseball is our thing. The kid'll play a game of catch until his arm falls off. Pretty good athlete, too. But the last few months have been different—for me anyway. Last spring Brian came down with a bad appendicitis. I removed his appendix. Found a tumor in his gut."

Abby squinted. "Is he sick?"

"No. Thank God. It was benign. I removed it and he's been checked every month since. No problems, but it scared the hell out of me. Brian's had a lot of health issues in his life. The last thing he needs is another. The kid is tough as nails. He's been through a lot and so far he's been indestructible. But I'm not sure my sister could handle anything else. Finding that tumor nearly sent her over the edge. It had an effect on me, too. That's when I had one of those life-is-too-short epiphanies. It sounds like such a cliché until you really understand the words. Life ends at some point, and you never know when that point is. So you better take advantage of each day."

He pointed to the slides where Brian was climbing the stairs again. They both waved up at him.

"So," Abby asked. "What does one do when they realize life is too short?"

"I'm not sure what other people do, but I decided to ask this girl I met at the gym out to dinner."

"Really?"

"Yep. She said yes, too, and we had a great time. But that was last spring. Haven't been able to figure her out since then."

Abby smiled and then wrinkled her nose. "Is she pretty?"

"Oh, yeah. You kidding me? A total knockout."

"Really?"

"No doubt. The problem is, I can't tell if she's interested."

"Yeah, girls can be weird like that sometimes."

"Tell me about it."

Abby moved her hand to the side of the table and pushed snow from the edge.

"She is, by the way." Their eyes met for an instant. "Interested," Abby said. "She's probably hard to read only because she's going through one of those epiphanies of her own and isn't quite through it yet. She's still trying to figure a few things out."

They stared at each other, not awkwardly, but the comfortable stare of two people on the outskirts of a relationship. Two people who had achieved great things through their careers but lacked the social graces that came so easily to others, both understanding their deficiencies stemmed from a troubled history rooted deep in their pasts.

"Uncle Joel! I'm going down!" Brian yelled from the top of the stairs.

Joel waved and watched his nephew bullet down the slide. "As much as he's going to protest, we've got to get going. I told my sister I'd have him home by nine. He's got a doctor's appointment tomorrow, so this was his little oasis away from all that stuff—scans and needles and bloodwork."

"You're a good uncle," Abby said. "And you're a pretty good date, too."

Chapter 31

Casablanca

Friday, November 10
7:42 p.m.

They dropped Brian off and waited until Joel's sister waved from the front door. Ten minutes later Joel pulled the Range Rover to the front of Abby's house.

"Thanks for tagging along," Joel said. "Brian had a good time with you."

"How about you?"

"Me too." He smiled. "It was a lot of fun. One of these days maybe I'll take you somewhere other than a work conference or out with my nephew. Maybe I could call you next—"

"Have you eaten?" Abby asked. "Because if you haven't, I could throw something together. Unless . . ."

"I'm starving," Joel said a little too quickly. "Would it be too much work?"

"I'm talking about pasta and marinara sauce, nothing special."

"Sounds perfect."

Half an hour later, they sat at the kitchen table with mounds of noodles in front of them. Abby opened a bottle of wine.

"I hope this is okay," she said.

Joel laughed. "Much better than I can do."

"The bachelor doesn't cook?"

Joel smiled. "I'm not even sure my oven works. Except the microwave."

They ate and refilled their wineglasses. Abby talked about Maggie and her folks. About her future nephew and how she, too, would be a godparent the way Joel was for his nephew. They talked about Brian and Joel's sister, Rachel. His oldest brother, Brandon, who lived an hour away and whose career as a thoracic surgeon consumed him much like Joel's did. Two busy physicians with hectic schedules was a great ruse to explain why Joel saw his brother only once a year, usually on Christmas. The truth—that the death of the middle Keaton boy had left an unbridgeable gap between Joel and Brandon—was a story for another time.

As the bottle of wine dwindled, they got to know each other, sharing stories from high school and college. It was one of those early conversations, the kind that shrinks time and turns hours into minutes; the kind that lays the foundation on which something greater might be built. Midnight crept up on them, and they were both surprised when they noticed the time. "Can you stay for a while?" Abby asked. "Or do you work tomorrow?"

"No, I'm off."

"We could throw on a movie?"

"I haven't watched a movie in . . . let's see, I took Brian last year to see—"

"You definitely work too much. Here, I have just the solution." Abby led him into the couch and grabbed a DVD from next to the television. "*Casablanca*?"

"I'll give it a shot."

"Give it a shot? It's a classic that gets better each time you watch it."

Joel raised his eyebrows. "Never seen it."

"Excuse me?"

"Never. Sorry."

"Move over," Abby said, climbing next to him on the couch. "I'll have to talk you through the beginning. It's important not to miss the little stuff."

"I hate movies I have to be talked through."

Abby dimmed the lights. "Not this one. This is not like other movies. There's lots of subtle things I'll have to point out." She looked at him with a serious expression. "You might cry."

"I doubt it."

"We'll see." She curled her legs into her chest as the movie started. "Now, pay attention. The beginning is important."

Curled in a nugget, watching a movie at midnight, Abby felt like a teenager. Until a few minutes into the movie, when she realized that the four trips down the hill and, more specifically, the three climbs back up, had drained her of energy. The bottle of wine wasn't helping, but there was something about *Casablanca* that kept her alert. The movie had a certain lure that stopped her from sleeping through it. Joel was another story. Just as Bogie was leaving for the first time, Joel's eyelids closed. His breathing settled into a deep rhythm, just on the edge of snoring.

Abby turned to see his eyes shut. She playfully elbowed him in the ribs.

"Can you believe she left him at the train station?"

Joel opened his eyes and cleared his throat, acting as though Bogie, standing there in the rain with his love letter, was riveting. "Unbelievable," he said. "You should never do that to a man." His eyes sagged again. He leaned deeper into the cushions and threw his arm over the back of the couch, behind Abby.

She smiled, curled herself tighter into a ball, and placed her head in the cul-de-sac of his shoulder and chest. She felt safe there, like she had when he wrapped his arms around her on their way down the slide. Abby watched the rest of the movie in the same position, listening to Joel's breathing and considering where life had brought her. She cried as the movie played, partly because she always cried when Bogie said good-bye to his true love, but mostly because Abby understood that she, too, was saying good-bye to a man she had loved her entire adult life.

Chapter 32

The Plan

Tuesday, November 21
11:00 a.m.

The churning stream snaked through the forest. The recent storms made its current robust and powerful. As he walked the banks he threw twigs onto the surface and watched the water whisk them away. His steps were slow and deliberate this morning as he worked out the logistics of his plan. The heavy weight of melancholy sagged his posture, as if his sadness were literally sitting on his shoulders. After thirty minutes he made it to the edge of the forest and approached the red cedar. From his pocket he removed the Swiss Army knife and unfolded the blade. Touching the tip to the smooth area on the trunk, he carved another notch into the wood and counted them again, like he'd done a hundred times before. Thanksgiving Day was approaching. His second on the island.

Ben sat on the ground with his back against the tree. He imagined his brothers gathered at his parents' house watching football. Stored deep in the folds of his mind were the smells of the season—cinnamon and nutmeg, stuffing and turkey. He thought of Abby and wondered if she still spent a portion of the holidays with his parents. A smile curled his lips when he remembered the terrible glögg wine his father-in-law forced him to drink each year. Memories of Thanksgiving and Christmas ran through his mind for some time before they settled. Then, sitting against the red cedar, Ben's thoughts shifted to another woman. He patted his slacks and pulled the crumpled letter from his pocket. The ocean had faded the ink from black to purple, but the words were still legible. He read the last sentence.

You need to tell your wife, Ben. She deserves to know the truth. I'll give you this week. Otherwise, I promise to tell her myself.

As he sat under his tree on his deserted island, Ben realized how far away he was from his wife, and how helpless he was to stop things. It had been a year and a half. Did Abby already know everything? He was a fool for not telling her when he had the chance. At least then he would have had the opportunity to explain things. Now Abby was living through it by herself. He closed his eyes and tried to push the nagging thoughts from his mind. Snapping twigs caught his attention, and when he opened his eyes he saw William approaching. The kid walked over to the tree and counted the last few marks Ben had carved.

"How close are we?" he asked in a deep, teenaged voice working its way to maturity.

Ben smiled. "Thanksgiving? It's either tomorrow or the next day. I might have missed a day, so I'm not certain."

William shrugged. "My dad was asking. I'll tell him it's in a couple of days. It'll give him something to look forward to."

"How's he doing?"

The kid shrugged. "Good days and bad days. But more

bad than good lately." He pointed over at his shack. "I should probably go check on him."

"Listen," Ben said. "I wanted to talk to you about our plan. I think I'm ready to get going."

The kid paused a moment. "Are you sure?"

Ben shrugged. "I'll never be sure. I've got a few things still left to do, but most everything is set."

The kid pointed to the backpack next to Ben.

"Your attitude changed after I found that journal."

Ben paused. "It reminds me how much I left behind, and how much my wife needs me to do this."

The kid nodded. "I have to be here for my dad."

"I know."

"How long will it take to finish the boat?"

Ben shook his head. "Not much longer, but I could use some help."

William was silent for a long time before he looked at Ben and smiled. "Okay. If you think it's time, then let's get you out of here."

Chapter 33

The Pilgrimage

Wednesday, November 22
1:30 p.m.

Christian Malone handpicked and secured twenty-two investors, and they all filled the conference room on the Wednesday before Thanksgiving. His financial advisors had pored over his business plan, his construction models, his timetables, and his list of investors. If he could raise the funds, the financial analysts, attorneys, and accountants who watched over his fortune would give their stamp of approval to move forward on his dream of creating an exclusive kitesurfing resort in the South Pacific.

He'd once believed that great wealth provided great freedom, and that was true at one point in his life. But strangely, once he achieved extreme wealth, his freedoms lessened. His company's IPO had turned him into a billionaire and brought less control to his life and his decisions. Everything he did was a reflection on the company, and he was required to always be on his best behavior. It was why he was always chasing the next success, and it explained his fascination with a tiny island in the South Pacific. If Christian could build this resort, perhaps he'd have a place to escape. Maybe he'd leave Silicon Valley behind, let the executives run his company and deal with his affairs. Or better yet, he'd allow them to buy him out and run him off so he could vanish and kitesurf his life away.

For an hour, Christian pitched his plans to his investors. He covered the buy-in proposal, the partnership structure, and the projected ROI over the next decade. Construction could begin as early as the following summer, with a completion date of eighteen months later. He hated numbers and pitches. He despised having to impress the people in this room. But he did it, and did it well, because he wanted this resort more than anything he'd ever wanted before.

"When do we get to see the island and the construction site in person?" one of the investors asked.

"Great question," Christian said. "I propose the first week of January. We'll get the holidays behind us, and then we'll all head down together. Let's say, January second? We'll fly on my corporate jet to Tahiti and spend the night. Then, the following morning, we'll take the floatplane out to the island and spend the morning touring the construction site. Our architectural team will join us, as well as our construction engineers."

"When was the last time anyone was on the island?" another investor asked.

"The last time any construction crews were there was just before Hurricane Earl hit, before we evacuated everyone. I went back a couple of weeks later to assess the damage, saw that it was a mess and not worth salvaging, so I shut things down. That was two years ago. Haven't been back since."

"How bad was it?"

"Not much damage to the land itself. The island is part of nature and has evolved to absorb hurricanes like Earl. But the early construction my crew accomplished—the temporary housing that was put up—was mostly destroyed. Luckily we were not far into construction, but just about everything that had been erected was lost."

"Are we worried about another storm erasing our investment?" another investor asked.

"Earl was terribly timed, and a once-in-a-generation storm. But I'm taking nothing for granted this time around. I've instructed the engineers to create building plans to reinforce the resort to handle a category five storm. The temporary housing that was put up was never meant to face a hurricane. Your investment is safe."

Christian looked around the room and watched his investors nod. They had faith in his plan.

"So," Christian said. "What do you say? Does January second work for everyone? We'll all head to the island to take a peek."

The room of wealthy investors made calls and plans, organized dates and moved meetings, and finally everyone agreed that the first week in January was when they would all take the pilgrimage to the small, secluded island in the South Pacific to see what the potential was and where their millions would be spent.

PART IV

A NEW YEAR

Chapter 34

Acceptance

Thursday, November 23
6:00 p.m.

Joel pulled the surgical cap from his head and threw it in the trash as he entered the doctors' lounge. It was 6:00 p.m. on Thanksgiving Day, and he'd been at the hospital for more than twenty hours. He had taken a call for another general surgeon and had an additional twenty-four hours of hospital coverage to go before he was free for the weekend. Things were quiet at the moment, but he was too tired to drive home. He climbed onto the bottom bunk in the doctors' lounge, sank his head into the pillow, and closed his eyes. He was asleep almost instantaneously.

The river raged as Joel dreamed. His brother clung to the fallen log while water crashed over his body. Joel's outstretched arm crept to within inches of his brother's, but would go no farther.

"I can't reach you," Joel said. "I need to get help."

"Don't leave me," his brother said.

"I'll get Dad."

"I can't hang on that long. Don't leave me."

Joel squatted on the rock and inched closer to the log, reaching again. Their fingers brushed, and Joel leaned farther. Their hands finally met, but before Joel could secure his hold on his brother's wrist, the raging water broke their grip. Joel watched as the river swallowed his brother downstream.

His mind jumped to his father's den, where he found himself staring through the bay window searching for deer. He longed to have his brother next to him, but there was something else congesting his sleeping mind. When he saw the man step from the cusp of the forest, it registered. In this dream, Joel had not been looking for deer but for the stranger, sensing that the man was a source for answers to questions that had haunted his life. Joel pushed through the squeaky patio door that led to the yard.

"Have you spotted any deer?" the man asked.

"No," Joel said. "I've watched for a long time. She's too scared."

"Keep looking. Don't give up. Sometimes the things we're searching for are right in front of us, but disguised by our thoughts and hidden by our fears, so we miss them. If you keep looking, though, and let go of the things you can't change, everything else disappears."

Joel stared at the man in front of him, considering his words before he looked off into the forest.

"I could have saved him. I could have told my dad that he needed help, but instead I just left him."

The man shook his head. "There are some things in life that we'll never make sense of. And if we're not careful, if we cling to the illusion that we could have changed the outcome, those moments from our past will stop us from finding happiness today. They'll stop us from seeing what's right in front of us. But acceptance can push us past it all. Acceptance of all the things that make no sense; acceptance of all the things we cannot change. Forgiving ourselves helps, too."

The man pointed into the trees.

"Don't give up on her. She wants you to find her."

The man turned, walked into the forest, and disappeared. A beeping noise emanated from the woods and became constant. It sounded like a dump truck set in reverse. Joel squinted into the forest, thinking perhaps it was the deer the man was talking about. Then he felt a hand on his shoulder. He turned his head.

"Dr. Keaton?"

Joel opened his eyes to see a nurse standing over him.

"Dr. Keaton, your pager is going off. They need you in the ER."

"I'm sorry," he said in a raspy voice. He sat up, fumbled with his pager, and turned it off. "I'll be right there."

Chapter 35

The Second Thanksgiving

Thursday, November 23
6:34 p.m.

On Thanksgiving Day the temperature sank to eleven degrees. Another eight inches of snow piled up on the frozen ground, and ice frosted the naked tree branches in a clear glaze. The early onset of winter kept people withdrawn and isolated inside their homes. At Thanksgiving dinner Abby displayed a similar withdrawal, which her parents attributed to another year without her husband. They didn't know that it was a different man who was on her mind tonight, one who had crept into a special place in her heart that she didn't know had room for anyone else.

When the dishes were cleared and the china replaced in the armoire, the family split into opposite directions. Abby's father and Jim headed to the couch to watch football. Abby's father had slightly altered the recipe for the upcoming Christmas glögg, still a month away, and wanted Jim's approval on the amendment. Mom headed to the den to call family, a long list she worked her way through each year. Maggie and Abby escaped to the living room. Abby had put together a baby shower the previous weekend and the sisters took inventory. They sorted through bags full of clothes and hats and socks and bibs and tried to comprehend the child who would soon fill them.

"It's crazy," Maggie said. "I've had three showers with one more to go. I don't know what to do with all this stuff."

"You'll need everything you get. The baby will grow out of these clothes in a few months. How do you feel?"

"Horrible. I can hardly get off the couch by myself, and getting out of bed in the morning is nearly impossible. I literally roll off the side. And I still have six weeks to go. I love this baby, but I want him out of me."

They cruised through the outfits and laughed at the tiny hats and two-inch socks.

"So what's happening with 'the doctor'?" Maggie asked, drawing out the word.

Abby shook her head. "I'm currently performing brain surgery on him."

"I don't get it."

Abby moaned. "I'm giving him mixed signals, not returning phone calls, and basically . . . I'm an idiot, Maggie. And I don't know what the hell I'm doing."

"What happened?"

"He stayed over a couple of weeks ago—"

Maggie, who had been reclined in a La-Z-Boy with baby paraphernalia sprawled over her ballooned stomach, karate-kicked herself upright and to the edge of the chair, eyes wide, and a huge grin on her face. "He stayed *overnight*?"

"Yeah."

"You slept with him!"

Abby made an ugly face. "No. He slept on the couch."

"Wait, what happened on the couch?"

"He *slept* on the couch, I slept in my bed."

"Oh," Maggie said, her forehead creased with disappointment. Her eyes were glazed in a remote stare. "I thought you were going to tell me something interesting for a second. About the couch and clothes flying and—"

"You're sad. Like, in a really demented, almost perverted way."

"It's been three months since I've had sex and at this rate—"

"Can I finish my story?"

"Right. I'm sorry." Maggie spun her index finger in tiny circles and rolled her eyes. "He's asleep on the couch."

"He's on the couch and I'm next to him and he's got his arm around me, and it feels . . ."

"Wrong?"

"No. It feels . . . perfect. Only . . . not perfect."

"Don't tell me. Ben shows up."

"I couldn't stop thinking of him."

"Thinking of him like you miss him, or thinking of him like you're guilty of something?"

"Both. I miss him *and* I feel guilty. Terribly, terribly guilty."

"Like you're cheating on him?"

"No, guilty like I'm moving on and . . . forgetting about him." Abby shook her head. "I like this guy, Maggie, and I am *so* screwing it up. And now that the holidays are here, it makes it worse. You know how nuts Ben was about Christmas—with presents for each of the twelve days of Christmas, the decorations, the massive Christmas tree he insisted we hunt for in Wisconsin and cut down fresh every year, the light show on Michigan Avenue. I think in the last few years that he actually started liking Dad's glögg wine. So anyway, it's hard when the season rolls around."

"I get it," Maggie said. "But what's been going on with Joel since the night he stayed over? Have you seen him?"

"After he spent the night, he sent a card and flowers telling me how much fun he had and that he was sorry for falling asleep."

"He fell asleep?"

"About ten minutes into *Casablanca*."

"And then sent flowers to apologize?"

"He's really good about cards and flowers."

"I've gotta meet this guy. Passes out during a date, *doesn't* sleep with you, and still has you raving about him."

Abby waved her off. "He called a couple days later and wanted to get together. But I was out of town for a few days, and then we had your shower. His schedule was full one weekend, so it brought us to Thanksgiving, which is when he asked me to have dinner with him. On Thanksgiving. I froze. I wanted to say yes. I mean, of course, I *wanted* to say yes, but something made me say no. I told him I couldn't disappoint Mom and Dad—like I'm a college kid home for Thanksgiving break." She shook her head. "That was last week. We haven't talked since. I'm such a wreck. Sooner or later he's going to give up. Or, I don't know, maybe he already has."

With a sigh, Maggie reclined back into her chair. "I know what you have to do, and I think you know, too." With her right arm she kicked up the footrest of the La-Z-Boy and groaned again until she was in a comfortable position. "You've gotta tell him about Ben."

Chapter 36

Better Late Than Never

Friday, November 24
7:00 p.m.

At seven o'clock on the Friday after Thanksgiving, Joel finally left the hospital. After Abby had turned down his invitation to Thanksgiving dinner he decided to work. A colleague had asked a month earlier if Joel would cover his call for the weekend. Joel received the request often; his doctor friends figured that with no wife or kids he would be happy to work every holiday while they all spent time with their families. The assumption typically bothered him, but this year Joel figured a busy night in the OR was better than a frustrating night at home trying to figure out why the first woman he had allowed himself to care for in over a decade was so hard to read.

His plan was a smashing success. The eve of Thanksgiving was always a busy night in emergency rooms, as the increased traffic on the roads brought in casualties from MVAs. He'd closed a number of lacerations, made a dozen surgical consults, and taken three trips to the operating room in the forty-eight hours between 7:00 p.m. the night before Thanksgiving and 7:00 p.m. the Friday after. Not once over the two-day span had he thought of Abby Gamble.

But on his way to his sister's house on Friday night, Abby crept back into his thoughts, and Joel realized that trying to avoid her magnetism was impossible. She pulled him in a way he'd never been pulled before. Joel was realizing that he didn't want to break free from it but was desperate to understand it. He sensed the mystery around her was not intentional. It was something she could not control, and he wondered what had happened in her past that caused her to be so guarded. She may have had her heart broken, although Joel couldn't imagine the idiot who would purposely cut Abby Gamble from his life. Or perhaps it was something else entirely. Something personal and private that she was not ready to share with him yet. Joel had some secrets of his own, and he was sure the last woman he had been close to—a surgical resident he'd met during his fellowship, with whom he had embarked on a turbulent two-year relationship—had agonized over his own lack of commitment as he sabotaged happiness to cater to his guilt. And now that Joel was on the receiving end of such treatment, he could see how his former girlfriend could have found that breakup years ago enigmatic and hard to understand.

When he pulled up to his sister's house, he wasn't any closer to finding answers to his relationship with Abby. He walked up the stairs and rang the bell. Brian answered a minute later.

"Better late than never. Thanksgiving was yesterday."

Joel nodded. "I told you I had to work."

"As usual," Brian said. "Mom saved some leftovers."

Brian held the door open, and Joel walked inside. "Thanks, buddy." He tousled Brian's hair.

"Hey, big brother," Rachel said as Joel walked into the kitchen. "Save any lives?"

"Yeah, just like Superman."

He gave Rachel a kiss on the forehead.

"Where's the little guy?"

"Already down for the night."

"Want me to wake him up?" Brian asked.

"Absolutely not," Rachel said. "Let your little brother sleep."

"But Uncle Joel won't get to see him."

"I'll come back tomorrow and see him," Joel said. He looked at Rachel. "How's Dad?"

Rachel shrugged. "Same. I went yesterday, spent about two hours with him. I told him it was Thanksgiving, and he opened his eyes for a second. That was about it."

"After I eat I'll head over and sit with him for a while tonight. Thanks for the leftovers."

In the kitchen, Brian put a plate of food in the microwave. "Anything bloody come into the ER?" he asked.

"Nah," Joel said. "Nothing too bad. Oh, actually, I take that back. There was one scalp laceration that was pretty nasty."

"Sweet! How many stitches?"

Rachel shook her head. "I'll let you boys get it out of your system." She walked out of the kitchen and into the living room.

"Eighteen," Joel said after Rachel was gone.

"What's your record?"

"For stitches? I once put fifty into someone's leg after they fell off a ladder and into a cast iron fence."

"Nice," Brian said as the microwave beeped. He removed the plate of leftovers and handed it to Joel.

"Thank you." Joel picked up a fork and started eating.

"How's Abby?"

Joel looked up from his food in mid-bite.

"Why are you asking?"

"Because she seemed nice."

Joel shrugged and went back to his food. "It's a long story."

"You're not screwing it up, are you, Uncle Joel?"

"I'm trying really hard not to."

Chapter 37

Molding

Wednesday, December 20
12:45 p.m.

Christmas fell on a Monday and Joel decided that this year an extended break was needed. He saw patients in his office until noon on Wednesday before his staff bolted for the exits on their way to a long Christmas weekend. It was the first time Joel had shut his office for so many straight days. He had blocked his call schedule at the hospital, and for the first time in many years he was staring at a few days free from work. He dictated the last of his charts and clicked off the office lights. He made rounds that afternoon on his hospitalized patients and wrote a few discharges. The process took three hours, and as he typed notes into the last of his charts a nurse approached him.

"Don't forget to see Sophie before you leave," she said.

Joel took the chart the nurse was holding and read the name. *Sophie Austin.* She was a six-year-old who'd had a perforated appendix removed the night before.

"She keeps asking if she'll get to go home for Christmas, and I keep telling her that it's up to you."

Joel shook his head. "A perfed appy? She'll be here another few days. We have to make sure there's not a rebleed or
a secondary infection. You know that."

"I do know that. But *you're* breaking the news to her,
not me."

"Help me out here?" Joel asked. "I'm up to my neck in
charts."

"No you're not," the nurse said. "Rumor has it you're taking a few days off for the first time ever. And I know the
chart you're working on is your last."

"What is this, the CIA around here?"

"No. But when Dr. Keaton decides to take time off, we all
notice, that's all. And I'm not telling Sophie and her mom
that she's here to stay for Christmas. This one's on you."

"Please?"

"No way," the nurse said. "She's crying because she thinks
Santa won't come to the hospital. I'm not telling her that she
has to stay."

Joel had always delegated kid-care to nurses or residents,
claiming he wasn't good with young patients. *Get 'em in, get
'em open, get 'em out. But get to know 'em on your own time.*

He tapped the keyboard and closed the chart. "Fine. I'll
take care of it. But next time an old guy needs a prostate
check, I'm calling you."

"Sophie's in room one fifty-three," she said and handed
Joel the chart.

"I hope you get coal in your stocking."

The nurse smiled. "Enjoy your time off. And if I don't see
you, have a merry Christmas."

"Yeah," Joel said, looking at the chart. "You, too."

After he finished his charting and orders, he entered room
153, where he found Sophie resting quietly under the covers.
Joel logged in to the bedside computer and reviewed her latest labs. As he typed, the young girl woke and gave a groggy

smile; her mother rose from the chair next to the bed and stretched.

"How's our patient doing?" Joel asked.

"She's doing pretty well," Sophie's mother said. "Eating a little. Mostly Jell-O."

"Good. Lots of fluids, too." Joel approached the bed. "I'm going to sit you up, sweetie, and check your stomach."

"Okay," Sophie groaned.

Joel peeled back the gauze and checked the incision. He palpated her midsection and then replaced the gauze. He placed his stethoscope on her abdomen. "Looks good, sounds good. Have you walked yet?"

"Yeah," Sophie said. "The nurses helped me this morning."

"Good. You're a strong little girl."

"Do I have to stay in the hospital for Christmas?"

Her mother smiled. She knew the answer.

"Yeah, sweetie," Joel said. "We need to keep you here for a few more days and make sure everything is healing and all your lab tests are normal before you go home. If we let you go home too soon, you'll end up right back here. But Christmas around this place is the best! The nurses make it lots of fun."

Sophie's eyes teared up. Her mother stroked her hair. "She's afraid Santa won't come to the hospital."

"Santa?" Joel asked. His forehead was wrinkled and his eyes were glazed with confusion. "Didn't the nurses tell you?"

Sophie shook her head.

"They didn't tell you? Hmm, maybe they were keeping it a secret." He leaned toward Sophie and whispered. "Santa comes every year to visit the kids in this hospital."

Sophie smiled, her eyes wide. "Every year?"

"Every year. He comes right into your room to give you a present. Special delivery."

"Even though there's no chimney in my room?"

"Even without a chimney."

"Are you sure?"

"Am I sure? I'm your doctor, of course I'm sure."

Sophie smiled at her mother.

"I've got to run, sweetie. The nurses will check on you again in about two hours, okay?" Joel looked at Sophie's mom. "She's doing great. I bet another week, at most."

Sophie's mom nodded and mouthed *thank you.*

"You guys have a merry Christmas," Joel said.

A few minutes later Joel pulled out of the hospital parking lot and, with some effort and the aid of his GPS, found the store he was looking for on Monroe. He parked on a side street and doubled back, pulling open the store door to chiming bells that were attached to it. Twenty minutes later he left with a Santa suit in a garment bag, which he hung in the back of his Range Rover.

He turned onto Lake Shore Drive and looked out at the icy shores of Lake Michigan. The beach was empty and desolate and snow-covered. The last year had undoubtedly changed Joel. He was taking long weekends. He was going out of his way to deal with his pediatric patients. And he was about to put himself far outside of his comfort zone, where he rarely ventured. He knew, somehow, that Abby Gamble was responsible for this molding. She was affecting every part of his life—making him better at everything he did.

Before he could change his mind, he stepped on the brake pedal and swung the Range Rover off LSD, taking the exit at the last second. He found Wacker Drive and took it west, then headed north on Michigan Avenue. He wasn't sure of the exact location, but as he crossed the river he knew he was getting close. When he reached the Magnificent Mile he slowed down, looking at each storefront window and checking addresses against the sheet of paper in his hand. He found it sandwiched between Tiffany and Pottery Barn. Traffic clogged every lane of Michigan Avenue, and Joel knew his next move would not be welcomed.

The Mag Mile drew twenty-two million visitors each year, and as Joel pulled to the curb and glanced in the rearview, he considered that all of them might be present that day. He double-parked and pushed on his hazards, drawing a cacophony of horns from the vehicles behind him, but he didn't care. He jumped out and headed across the sidewalk, which was filled with Christmas shoppers in organized herds heading north and south. He peered through the window and saw that the place was packed. Mariah Carey's "All I Want for Christmas Is You" spilled out into the cold air as he opened the door and slipped inside.

The salon was two stories high, with an open atrium that allowed the activity on the second floor to be viewed by those browsing the main gallery. There were fifteen chairs on the upper-level veranda, all occupied by women being tended to by stylists applying makeup and primping hair. It was bright upstairs, with mirrors on each wall that made the place seem to go on and on. The lower level was a city of backlit glass shelves holding perfectly organized cosmetic products. Women carried bags and browsed the shelves.

"Can I help you find something?" a young woman asked.

Joel sensed the sales assistant was used to confused and overwhelmed men walking through the doors and into this foreign land of makeup and skin care and hair products.

"Yes. Is Abby Gamble around?"

"She's in her office. Can I tell her who's asking?"

"Joel."

"Can I tell her what it's concerning?"

Joel thought for a second. "Um, sure. It's about Christmas."

The young woman smiled. "Okay," she said, nodding as if his answer made perfect sense. She headed up the stairs. Joel shot a look out the front window to check on the Range Rover. A Chicago PD squad car had just rolled up behind him. The red and blue lights flicked on.

"I didn't see your name on the schedule for a facial," Abby said. She was leaning over the glass railing on the upper level.

Joel smiled. "I think my pores are clogged."

Abby laughed and held up her index finger. "Hold on, I'll be right down."

Joel watched as she spoke with an assistant, then signed a document another woman brought to her. On her way past her customers in the salon chairs, she smiled and touched a few on the shoulder while admiring the work. Joel started to sweat as the cop tried the driver's-side door of the Range Rover and, finding it locked, cupped his hands and peered into the vehicle. The officer grabbed the radio from his shoulder.

"Hey," Abby said when she made it down the stairs.

Joel held out his arms. "I'm officially impressed," he said. "You've got eighteen of these?"

Abby shrugged. "Just a girl with a dream. Listen, I'm sorry I haven't called, or returned calls. As you can tell, it's been a little crazy around here with the Christmas rush. And, well . . . Christmas gets me out of sorts."

"Apology accepted. Look, I don't have a lot of time." Joel pointed over his shoulder to the street.

Abby looked through the front window. "Is that your car?"

"It is."

"Double-parked on Michigan Avenue? At Christmastime. Are you insane?"

"I'm starting to think so, yes."

The squeaking brakes and yellow flashers of a tow truck caught their attention.

"Damn!" Joel turned back to Abby. "I've gotta go. Listen,

the reason I stopped by . . . Do you have plans on Christmas Eve?"

Abby looked confused by the question. "For . . . when?"

"Christmas Eve. You know, the day before Christmas."

"Actually, I don't."

"Good. I want to spend it with you."

She smiled, slowly nodding her head. "Okay. We should do that."

He was shocked he had gotten it out, and that she had agreed so easily. Surprised that he was standing here in the first place when he had begun his day with no plans to make such an offensive.

"Okay then," he said. "I'm glad we worked that out." He pointed over his shoulder. "I should probably go."

Abby tried not to laugh. "You'd better hurry."

"I'll see you on Christmas Eve?"

"Yes."

"There's no backing out once I leave."

"Understood."

"I won't answer my phone if you call to cancel."

"Go! Before they impound you."

Joel walked backward for a few steps. "You look good when you're at work."

"They're going to tow you."

"Professional but relaxed. In control but not domineering."

"Go, you fool!"

He turned and ran out the door. He approached the officer with his hands raised. Horns continued to sound. Joel shrugged his shoulders and opened his palms at a cab driver who swerved around him and extended a finger out the window.

"Totally unnecessary," Joel yelled as the cabbie sped past. "But completely justified."

When he looked back to the storefront, he saw Abby

watching him from inside. She was doubled over with laughter as she watched the scene he had caused on Michigan Avenue. Joel laughed too as the police officer began scolding him. As he stood in traffic and listened to the horns and the yelling, he realized that somehow during the past year, he had fallen in love.

Chapter 38

Rocks

Wednesday, December 20
4:20 p.m.

Behind the shacks stood a shed filled with tools and lumber. Ben had found it long ago, and whoever had once been to this island had started setting up a workshop for whatever it was they were planning to build. Ben had used the tools to shore up the two shacks he and William had occupied since their arrival on the island. The supplies had always whispered to Ben. In them he saw opportunity. In the timber and the tools he imagined a boat that could carry them away from that place. He saw it perfectly in his mind and longed for the day he might sit in the boat and push off from shore.

He stood next to the wood he had gathered and contemplated the best way to finish his boat, which rested on the ground, mostly built and leaning to the starboard side. As he gathered wood, he saw William standing out in the surf. The kid was side-arming rocks and skipping them along the ocean's surface. Ben dropped the wood and headed toward the beach. He watched for a minute while William continued to throw.

"You've got a pretty good arm."

William looked back. "Thanks."

"How old are you?"

"Sixteen."

"You play any sports?"

"I pitched on my high school baseball team."

"It shows."

William threw another rock. "How's the boat coming?"

Ben walked out into the surf until the ocean reached his calves and he was standing next to the kid.

"Almost finished."

William threw another stone and they both watched it skip across the water.

"How's your dad doing?" Ben asked.

The kid looked over, shook his head. "He's struggling."

Ben had worked together with the kid ever since the plane crash. After they had emerged from the forest to survey the wreckage, William brought Ben to his father, who was in bad shape then and had only gotten worse since.

"Is there anything I can do for him?"

"You can keep your promise," William said.

Ben looked out at the horizon and the many miles of ocean in front of him. He hoped it wasn't too late. "I will, don't worry about that. You just help your dad."

The kid threw another rock.

"You trust me, don't you?" Ben asked. "To help you and your dad? To go through with the plan?"

"After the plane crash," William said, "I knew you were the only person who *could* help me. So, yeah, I trust you." He looked at Ben. "Do you trust yourself?"

Ben shrugged. "I don't know. I won't know until I get there."

Ben reached into the water and scooped up a handful of rocks from the sand, turned to the ocean and tossed one.

"How old was your son when he died?" William asked.

The question caught Ben off guard.

"That's what's in the journal, right? Letters to your son?"

Ben nodded. "Yeah. They were letters I wrote to him after he died. Letters about his mother and me and how we met and how much I loved her."

Ben threw a second rock along the surface.

"He was just a few months old when he died."

The kid stared at the ripples in the water where Ben's rock had skipped. "That's sad."

"I stopped thinking of it that way. I had to or I never would have survived. I think about him all the time. I never got to know him the way most fathers know their sons. But it's funny—I imagine the times we should have had together. The friendship we would have developed. I think about picking him up and having him wrap his arms around my neck." Ben pitched another rock and watched it glide along the water.

"I think of his first step. His first word. His first day of school. His first everything has passed through my mind at some point. In my imagination, we've been everywhere together. Sometimes when I sleep I get to see him in my dreams. Some are so real I don't want to wake. I have to imagine what he looks like and sounds like. I have to create his smile and his laugh in my mind because I never got to see them. So in a strange way, I think I know him better than most fathers know their sons because I've had to create it all rather than witness it."

"So the letters, what, sort of helped you move on?"

"The letters were a way for me to heal. I couldn't find another way to reach him, so I started writing letters to him. Somehow writing those letters and creating that journal saw me through the pain of losing him."

William threw another rock. "Do you have other kids?"

Ben hesitated a moment, realizing how hard it was to answer the question. Realizing that perhaps his greatest regret in life had been refusing to have another child with Abby. Finally, he shook his head. "No. Just my son."

"You never tried to have another child?"

Ben rubbed his tongue against the inside of his lower lip and shook his head. "No."

"How come?"

Ben shrugged. "I don't really know. I was too scared, I guess. After a couple of years Abby wanted to try, but I couldn't. Only recently have I realized how selfish that was. And now I'm not sure I can do anything about it."

"Sure you can. It's never too late for anything. That's what my dad always used to tell me. We have a plan, and all you need to do is stick to it."

They chucked rocks, neither of them talking for a long time. In the background, the massive structure of the downed airplane dwarfed them. William dropped a few rocks into the water, sorting the stones in his palm until he found two smooth ones. He kept one and gave the other to Ben.

"I don't think my dad's got a lot of time. Let's get that boat finished so you can be on your way. Can I help you?"

Ben nodded. "Sure. I need all the help I can get."

The kid took his perfect stone and skipped it out into the ocean. Ben did the same.

Chapter 39

Ornaments

Sunday, December 24
10:34 a.m.

The morning of Christmas Eve was cold and windy, but the sky was a deep, cloudless blue. The sun was bright and shone through the window to slant across the tree that stood in the living room. Ornaments hung from the branches among colored lights. Decorating the tree had been a struggle, one Abby hadn't taken on the year before. Attached to every ornament were memories of Ben. Halfway through the process, Abby had found a clear crystal-ball ornament flecked with glitter. Laminated inside was a picture of her and Ben on their wedding day. He wore a tuxedo and she a white dress that went on forever.

She cried when she held it because she knew she couldn't hang it that year. Because she knew it would be harder to hang that ornament than to store it in the separate box she had prepared. She wrapped the crystal ball in tissue, putting a heavy extra layer around it, and placed it into the box labeled "old ornaments." It was the first ornament that went into the separate box. Others followed as she decorated the tree, separating out the ones that were particularly troubling and placing them into the box that would lie dormant in her basement. She laughed, too, as she hung others. There were a few godawful pieces that had crept down from generations past, and others that she had made as a child, when macaroni and Elmer's glue were considered decorative in schools around the country.

As she rummaged through the last of the ornaments she found one she hadn't expected. It caught her off guard; she hadn't seen it for two years. The flat, gold-plated rocking horse shone as though it were brand new, hiding the fact that it was more than a decade old. She ran her thumb over the name engraved on the saddle.

Jacob.

Her mother had given it to her for Christmas many years ago, when Abby was still pregnant. It was meant to be a tradition: Abby's mother planned to give all her grandchildren rocking horse ornaments with their names etched on the saddle, the same way Abby's grandmother had done for her.

Abby cried when she first found the ornament. But on the morning of Christmas Eve, as sunlight fell onto the rocking horse while it hung from the tree, it shone with hope and promise and made Abby smile. There were some things she needed to move on from, and other things she would never forget.

"I'm sure," Abby said, sitting at the kitchen table and talking into the phone.

"You're not sitting at home again, Abby. That's what you did last year and, quite frankly, it was a bummer for all of us," Maggie said. "Just come over to Jim's parents' house. There's plenty of room, and they'd love to have you. They told me to invite you."

"Thanks, Maggie, but I'm going to pass. I'll be at Mom and Dad's tomorrow. Bright and early."

"You know what? I'm not taking no for an answer. Jim's picking you up at five."

"No, he's not."

"Jim!" Maggie yelled. Abby heard her brother-in-law in the background. "You're picking Abby up tonight before we go to your parents'." Abby heard Jim give a response. "Done," Maggie said. "He'll be over at five."

"I won't be here."

"He'll wait for you, then."

"I don't know when I'll be home."

"Oh, stop it, Abby. Just come with us tonight."

"Maggie! I'm going out tonight."

"Sure. On Christmas Eve? Knock it off. It's—"

"Maggie." Abby pulled out the slow and calm voice again. It always worked. "I'm going out with Joel."

There was a slight pause.

"Get. Out!" Maggie said. "I thought you hadn't talked to him since before Thanksgiving."

"He stopped at the store the other day. Asked me to spend Christmas Eve with him."

"Are you meeting his parents?"

"No. We're doing something quiet. Just the two of us."

"Why didn't you tell me?"

"I don't know. I'm freaked out about it. I'm excited but still a little . . . it's Christmas, you know. I'm a lunatic this time of year."

"Yeah, well . . . get over it! And have fun. You deserve to have fun on Christmas. And tomorrow, I want to hear everything. Call me as soon as he leaves in the morning."

Abby rolled her eyes. "Good-bye, Maggie."

Chapter 40

The Lights

Sunday, December 24
5:00 p.m.

At five o'clock on Christmas Eve her doorbell rang. When she answered, the cold night air whistled into the foyer. Joel stood on the porch wearing a Santa hat.

"Ho, ho, ho."

Abby grabbed his hand and pulled him through the doorway. "Get in here. It's freezing out there." She slammed the door closed. "Are we really going out in this weather?"

"We really are," Joel said. He leaned toward her and kissed her cheek. "Merry Christmas."

With their faces close together, Abby brushed the snow off his shoulders. "Nice hat."

"Thank you."

"You're still not telling me where we're going?"

"Nope. But dress warmly. We might have to walk a little tonight."

"Any hints?"

"Somewhere cold."

"That narrows it down. You like surprises, don't you?"

"This one's hard to describe. But I know you'll like it." Joel looked at his watch. "But we better go. It'll be crowded."

"Crowded, huh?" Abby opened the closet and pulled her jacket off the hanger. "Ice skating on State Street?"

"Nope. Way too cold for that."

"The lights on Michigan Avenue?"

"Close."

"The Macy's window display?"

"You were closer before."

"Navy Pier?"

He rolled his eyes. "Now you're way off. Let's go."

They took the Kennedy Expressway heading north out of the city. When the expressway forked a few minutes later they followed I-94 west. After a few miles they exited and drove the back roads. When Joel turned the Range Rover off the two-lane street and into a residential neighborhood, they ran into traffic. In the dark, the red brake lights aligned like rush hour. Up ahead, Abby saw the glow of houses. She squinted to get a better look, but they were too far off.

"What's up there?"

"Christmas lights. It's a little neighborhood that's unbelievable. Every house outdoes the next. I haven't been here for years. I hope nothing's changed."

They followed the bumper-to-bumper traffic until they finally reached the neighborhood where they drove past houses ridiculously decorated. Lights covered trees and bushes. They outlined rooftops and garages. Christmas trees filled windows; nativity scenes occupied lawns. Santas and snowmen stared down from chimneys. Abby was amazed.

"This is nothing. Just a little appetizer," Joel said. "Wait until we get there."

Five more minutes of crawling and they finally arrived. The street they were on bled into a wide loop that encircled a ten-acre park. The park was dark, but the houses surrounding it were ablaze with Christmas decorations. Lights of every color flashed and blinked. Not only trees and bushes and gutters, but rooftops and windows also glowed. The lights reached the tops of trees that were three stories high. Nativity scenes came to life with characters seven feet tall and mangers made from thick wood and filled with hay. The rooftops of houses held reindeer harnessed to Santa's sleigh. Ten-foot Santas were everywhere, their arms and necks rotating in robotic rhythm. Snow covered the ground and was piled high at the sides of driveways and sidewalks. People walked as though window-shopping, the magic of the season and the majestic setting protecting them from the cold.

Joel pulled over and parked. "What do you think?"

"I think it's amazing." Abby looked through the windshield. "I've never seen anything like it."

"I haven't been back here since I was a kid," Joel said, also peering through the windshield. He was staring into his past, and he knew coming here was the only way to address a long-ignored problem. The last time he had seen this neighborhood and the lights was nearly thirty years ago, the Christmas before his brother drowned in the Pichatauk River. So many things had changed since that day. That his family never again ventured out on Christmas Eve to see the lights was no mystery. His brother had loved the tradition too much for his parents to return.

"Come on," Joel finally said. "Let's walk."

Abby zipped her coat to her chin and sank her hands into her mittens. Joel took her hand. They walked past one of the nativity scenes and had to look up to see the faces of the wise men. They walked past driveways lined with candy canes— hundreds of them bordering the yard and running up the drive. Lighted soldiers, lined in perfect rows along the sidewalk and glowing bright, guarded another house. They passed a carousel where reindeer circled, and music chimed.

Garage doors were wrapped in shiny green paper with giant bows across the front. Making a loop around the park, they slowed as they approached a house on the north end.

"This used to be my favorite when I was a kid," Joel said.

They stopped in front of a two-story house whose massive double-decker bay windows were filled with a giant Christmas tree, the base of which took up the bottom window with the middle portion filling the window on the second story. The tip of the tree finally emerged on the rooftop—a giant Christmas tree that took up two levels and popped through the roof.

"It must look awful from the inside," Joel said, "As kids my brothers and I always wondered how they fit the tree into the house. My dad used to tell us it had to be specially delivered by helicopter and that the roof was temporarily removed to set it up." Joel smiled as he stared at his childhood, his thoughts taking him across the years. "Man, we used to eat it up. Rachel, who was the youngest of all of us, always laughed at my father's explanation. She knew it was a con. But my brothers and I, we couldn't get enough."

Abby stared at the tree that sprouted through the roof and then looked at Joel. Joel felt her gaze on him. He smiled.

"What?"

"I've never seen you like this," she said.

"It's been a long time since I've been back here. It brings back a lot of memories."

He put his arm around her as they stared at the lights. He felt Abby put her arm around his waist and rest her head on his shoulder.

"Is it the same as last time you were here?" she asked.

He pulled her tight. The last time he was here was with his brother. But Abby's presence by his side filled a void that might otherwise have swallowed the joy of coming back here.

"No. It's different. But it's still really good."

* * *

They opened a bottle of wine at Abby's place, and while Christmas carols played in the background, they stirred shrimp that was frying on the stove. Bobby Helms's "Jingle Bell Rock" hit the speakers while Abby lit candles on the dining room table. Joel carried in the bowl of shrimp, and they sat and ate.

"So what do you normally do on Christmas Eve?" Joel asked.

"Oh, sometimes my parents', sometimes my sister's. It depends." The answer was short and brief and a total lie. Abby had spent the last fifteen years with Ben's parents and had spent last year alone. This year she hadn't even talked to her in-laws. Abby thought of telling Joel everything right there at the dinner table. Joel's question was the perfect segue. But instead she smiled.

"How about you?"

"It used to be my parents' every year, but since my brother and sister have had kids, the night has migrated to their houses. They take turns. I went to Brandon's house last year. This year everyone is at Rachel's."

"I hope you don't get any grief for not showing up."

"Oh, I'm sure Brian will give me an earful. But I told him I was spending the night with you, and he gave me his approval. He likes you."

"That's sweet."

"How about you? Are you taking heat for not going to your parents'?"

"A little. But it's the same story with Maggie. As soon as she heard I was spending the night with you, she was all for it."

"For what it's worth," Joel said, "this has been a lot nicer. And much quieter."

"I think so, too." She smiled. "I loved the lights."

"Maybe we can do it again next year. Turn it into a new tradition."

"I'd like that." She reached across the table and took his hand. "Let's go open presents."

Joel nodded. "I think I did pretty good with yours."

"I guarantee you'll like yours," Abby said. "I cheated, though, and got some outside help."

In the living room, Abby took a gift bag from half dozen presents that were scattered under the tree. "Merry Christmas."

Joel shook the bag lightly. He removed the red tissue paper and pulled an envelope from the bag. The Chicago Cubs logo was printed on the outside. Inside were two tickets to the winter Cubs convention—where fans meet the players and hear about the upcoming season. Memorabilia was autographed and photos were taken.

"This is great. I didn't know you liked baseball."

"I don't. The other ticket is for Brian. I did some recon while we were tobogganing."

"No wonder he was so excited for me to spend the night with you. Sure you don't want to come? We could get another ticket."

"Baseball? I'd rather sit through another dinner conference on gastric bypass."

"Ouch."

"Most boring sport ever invented." She pointed to the bag. "There's something else. It's on the bottom."

He fished through the tissue paper and found a thin rectangular box wrapped in gold. He tore off the paper and smiled, then sank his head in embarrassment as he held up a DVD of *Casablanca*.

"It's the seventy-fifth anniversary collector's edition," Abby said.

"I'll make sure I watch the whole thing next time. Promise."

"At least get past the first ten minutes."

He leaned over and kissed her. It lasted just a second but felt much longer to Abby. His lips were soft and full, like they had been the first time. She put her hand to his cheek now, the way she had a few weeks before when they stood on her doorstep, but this time she leaned forward and kissed him again.

Her eyes were closed, and this time she had no intention of ending things. Then she felt Joel pull away.

"Your turn," he said.

Joel grabbed a haphazardly wrapped gift from beneath the tree.

"Sorry. I've never been very good at wrapping presents."

"You can stitch abdomens back together but you can't wrap a present?"

"It's an affliction."

Abby peeled away the wrapping paper to find a framed picture of the two of them taken from a camera mounted halfway down the toboggan slide. Abby's eyes were shut and her face was a combination of excitement and terror. Joel's chin was on her shoulder, his eyes wide open. Engraved on the stainless-steel frame were the words: *I've got you.*

Abby remembered how he had whispered those words in her ear. Panic had gripped her as they'd stared down the long, icy slide. But his words had taken her fear away. She remembered the feel of his arms around her.

I've got you.

"I love it," she said, staring at the two of them in the photo. "God, I was scared."

"It shows."

Abby laughed. "Oh my God, I was petrified!"

Joel leaned over to get a better look. He laughed, too. "We look good together."

"Yeah, we do."

She kissed him again. "Thank you."

Joel smiled. "I'll help you clean up."

They picked up the wrapping paper and loaded dishes into the dishwasher.

"It's getting late," Joel said. "I'd better get going."

"Don't tell me you're working on Christmas Day."

"Technically, no. But Santa *is* making an appearance at the hospital early tomorrow morning. I promised a six-year-old girl that the fat man in the red suit would make a special delivery to her room on Christmas morning."

Abby smiled. "Don't tell me."

"Yep, I'll be Santa Claus tomorrow morning on the pediatric floor. Did you know a Santa suit costs six hundred bucks?"

"What? Why didn't you rent it?"

Joel shrugged. "I figured I'd make it a yearly tradition at the hospital. Maybe stop at my brother's house afterward. I don't see his kids enough. It's one of my New Year's resolutions to make a bigger effort to see Brandon more this coming year. He's got a three-year-old and a six-year-old. I figure I'm safe with the three-year-old. The older one will probably blow my cover the second I walk in the door."

"I'm sure they'll be thrilled. I bet your brother will be, too."

They walked into the foyer. Abby took his coat off the banister and handed it to him.

"Thanks for taking me to see the lights. It was really . . . special."

She wanted to say that she'd remember it forever. She wanted to tell him that it was a Christmas she desperately needed. That last Christmas was a mess, and this one was nearly perfect. She wanted to ask him to stay, to curl up on the couch next to the fire and stare at the tree and listen to Christmas music. And she wanted to kiss him again. As she stood in front of him, though, something stopped her.

"Merry Christmas," she said.

"Merry Christmas."

Joel opened the door.

"Say hi to Brian for me."

"I will."

He backed out of the doorway and slowly pulled the door closed. Abby took a deep breath and blew out a lungful of air that ricocheted off her bottom lip and fluttered the front of her hair. She went back to the living room and picked up the picture. She ran her hand over Joel's face, then placed it on the mantel next to the picture of Ben and his father on their fishing trip, the only picture of Ben that remained.

She sank into the couch and remembered the previous year, when she sat in the same place on the same night and thought of a different man while she cried over letters and greeting cards. Now she was stuck in the middle, between two perfect men. Not far enough removed from one, not close enough to the other.

Chapter 41

The Second Christmas

Monday, December 25
10:12 a.m.

He made his way to the red cedar that stretched high into the forest. The vine, which had been thin and barren when Ben first came upon the tree, was now thick and sturdy. It climbed high into the tree's limbs and hugged the jagged face of the trunk, where a lightning strike had peeled away the bark. He took hold of the vine. It was as broad as the barrel of a Louisville Slugger, and it occurred to Ben how long he'd been there. When he'd first arrived, the vine was thin and wispy, and its metamorphosis told him it was time to go. He had made a promise to William, and he was going to keep it. He'd already done a great deal of work to that end but needed to do a little more before they said good-bye. Ben used the Swiss Army knife to carve another notch into the tree trunk, and then he counted. It was Christmas Day.

Near the edge of the forest, Ben found his coconut tree. It was the one he had decorated the year before with wild berries and a fossilized starfish. The single frond had grown taller and stronger since the previous year and was able to support more ornaments this time around. Ben remembered Jacob's rocking horse ornament that he and Abby hung from their tree each year. The memory was enough to get him moving now. He walked out of the forest, past the wreckage of the airplane, and to the shed beyond it, whose barn-style doors were open wide. Lumber was piled to the side, stacked ten feet high and in perfect rows. He had used most of it to construct his boat, a sturdy vessel he was sure would do the trick.

The son of a man who callused his hands with manual labor, Ben had once found solace in craftsmanship. Building and creating came naturally to him. He had always been able to visualize from random pieces of material the final product of his craft. And now the unmarred lumber stacked and waiting, the tools hanging from the walls of the shed, filled him with a sense of wonder and an eagerness to finish his project. The hope stored in the materials had gotten him this far; the idea of finding his way back to Abby took him the rest of the way.

He took a fresh plank of wood from the top of the stack and laid it across the logs he used as a workbench. He put the blade of the saw to the wood and felt sawdust mist into the air as he pulled back and forth. At the edge of an uninhabited beach that welcomed the water's edge, Ben Gamble stood next to the ravaged plane that had delivered him to this place, hammering nails and sawing lumber. He was back in a familiar place of craftsmanship that reminded him of his father and of his youth, and as long as his hands touched the wood and throbbed under the tension of the saw, thoughts of his wife and how badly he missed her on Christmas Day were manageable. Because soon, he knew, he'd see her again.

Chapter 42

Resolutions

Sunday, December 31
10:45 a.m.

On the morning of New Year's Eve, the woman pulled her car to the curb outside Abby Gamble's house. It was the third time she'd come. The first was months earlier, when she sat in the car with her infant son and watched Ben's widow turn off lights as she readied for bed. The second was before Thanksgiving, when she had actually gained enough courage to approach Ben's wife with his letter in her hand. She had been so close that day to handing over Ben's letter and getting it all out in the open. But something stopped her, and she raced back to her car and drove off before she had told Abby Gamble anything about the secret she shared with Ben. On this morning, she arrived at the house knowing she would not go inside. Today's trip was to fortify her resolution. New Year's Eve was not the right time. But she had made a decision and placed the date on the calendar. She could not go another year with her secret. She couldn't endure another year without telling Abby Gamble the truth.

The New Year had always been a time for resolutions. A time for fresh starts and new challenges. A time to take action. As soon as the new year arrived, she planned to finally knock on the front door of the house and have a long-overdue talk with Ben's wife.

Chapter 43

Happy Birthday

Sunday, December 31
5:42 p.m.

The annual New Year's Eve party at the Renaissance hotel originally consisted of college friends and work colleagues, but over the years it had grown and swelled and was finally capped at two hundred. The largest ballroom was reserved each year, with formal seating to accommodate one hundred fifty; more guests would arrive after dinner. A band played slow music while entrees were served and livened things up afterward. Maggie and Jim had been organizing the event for a decade, and many had wondered during the months leading to New Year's if the party would take place this year, with Maggie nearly nine months pregnant. But she forced Jim to proceed, even if she had little chance of making it to midnight.

Abby had been absent the previous year, too consumed with the grief of the past year to celebrate the one before her. But things were different now; Abby was looking forward instead of backward, and her preparation was an all-day event. In nothing but her bra and bikini-style bottoms, she fine-tuned her makeup. She'd spent the afternoon at her salon with her top makeup artist, who took advantage of AG Cosmetics' full line of toner, foundation, blush, mascara, and lipstick to get Abby ready for the evening. Abby had spent two hours in the chair while her employee tried different combinations of lipsticks and highlights. She went through several different hairstyles before settling on a deep side part with her hair curled in a long wave that fell over her left shoulder. She pinched and pruned the ends now as she stood in her bathroom and stared into the mirror. Her mani-pedi from that morning was flawless, and she gave her hair one last light coat of spray.

The pampering ended a half hour before Joel was to pick her up. In a final push, Abby opened the windows and allowed the December air to fill the bedroom. Once her body temperature was at the correct degree of frigidness, she closed the windows and snaked into her evening gown—a black Renee Bardot that hugged her hips, with spaghetti straps and a plunging neckline.

She looked in the mirror and admitted to her reflection that she looked damn good. Her shoulders spanned out horizontally and the tiny straps of her dress ran over her clavicles like fine streams running down a mountainside. The dress pinched her thin waist before flowing over her hips and ending just above her toned calves, which were on display tonight, courtesy of the sharp slant of her high heels. Abby wondered how long she'd last in them.

She touched Chanel N°5 to her neck while her stomach did somersaults. The doorbell rang just as she applied a highlighting coat of lipstick. She headed down the stairs and opened the door.

"Wow," Joel said from the front porch. She watched his eyes wander for a second. "You look stunning."

"Thank you. Come on in. We can have a drink before we

leave, but we need to get there a little early. I don't think Maggie'll make it very long tonight, and I want to make sure you meet her and that we get to spend some time together."

She took Joel's trench coat. He was wearing a crisp charcoal suit that complemented his temples, with a navy blue tie. His broad shoulders filled the suit, and the sharp angle of his jaw gave him a sturdy look that Abby had grown fond of. When he handed Abby his coat, she stopped and stared. Longer than the subtle glance he had taken. Something came over her, a sensation of curiosity and anticipation she was sure originated with how things had ended on Christmas Eve—when Joel left despite her desire for him to stay.

She remembered him backing through the doorway on Christmas Eve. She remembered nearly asking him to stay but failing to locate the words. Without thinking now, she took a step closer, reaching for his coat with one hand and placing the other on his chest until her hand was the only thing separating their bodies. Then she tapped into the extra half inch that remained in her tiptoes. She kissed him, his lips as soft as they were a week ago. The kiss lingered for a bit, and when their lips finally separated, they stared at each other.

"You look really handsome."

Abby let herself down from her tiptoes and backed away with Joel's jacket in her hand. She turned and opened the closet.

"How far along is she?" Joel asked.

Her mind was still congested from the kiss. "How far is what?"

"Maggie. How far along?"

"Oh, um, eight and a half months. Give or take a week or so. She's ready to pop."

She stared at him again. Joel grinned and raised his brows in expectation. "How 'bout that drink?"

"Right." Abby turned and headed for the kitchen. She closed her eyes on the way and suppressed the smile that was pushing its way onto her face.

They valeted the Range Rover and walked up the steps of the Renaissance hotel. Joel took her hand as they rode the elevator to the third floor where the Looking Glass Ballroom was slowly filling with guests. The lights of the city spilled through the floor-to-ceiling windows that looked down over the Chicago River. Abby spotted Jim and Maggie huddled near a group of people by the bar. She led Joel over and tapped her sister on the shoulder. Maggie turned around, her giant belly leading the way.

"Oh my God, I hate you," Maggie said, her face serious and smoldering as she stared at Abby. "Look how thin you are. God, I can't believe I used to look like you." Maggie shook her head. "Why are you wearing a dress like that when I'm stuck in this absurd outfit?"

Maggie was wearing a red dress that hugged her inflated stomach.

"Stop it," Abby said. "All nine-months-pregnant women should look so good."

"Go eat some ice cream or have a burger or something."

"Maggie, this is Joel," Abby said. "Joel, this is my sister, Maggie."

"Hi, Maggie. Your sister talks about you all the time." Joel leaned over and gave Maggie a hug. "And I think you look great."

Maggie stared at Joel like a high school girl giggling at a good-looking teacher. She stared, unblinking, and was silent for several seconds before she finally said, "I'm usually thirty pounds lighter."

Abby raised her eyebrows. "Thanks for that bit of important information. Maggie, he knows you're pregnant."

"My ankles are swollen so I can't wear high heels. I usually look taller than this."

Abby looked at Maggie's feet and noticed flip-flops that indented her swollen skin.

Maggie rattled off another. "I've also retained water in my face, so my cheeks look heavier than normal. I have high cheekbones, just like her."

Abby's brow remained pinched as she listened to her sister. "Again, he gets it. You're pregnant."

"I have to go to the bathroom," Maggie said, in the same rapid, robotic voice. "That's another thing. I have to pee constantly." She finally pulled her gaze from Joel and looked at Abby. "I need you to come with me."

Abby looked at Joel with a bizarre smile. "I'll be right back."

"Good luck," Joel said.

"This is my husband, Jim." Maggie grabbed Jim by the shoulder and spun him away from the couple he was talking to. "Jim, Joel. You guys talk. Or get a drink. Or, you know, do guy stuff for a while."

Maggie dragged Abby towards the bathroom. Halfway there, Abby looked at her.

"What the hell's the matter with you?"

"What?"

"I'm usually forty pounds lighter? My ankles are swollen? My face is bloated?"

"First of all, it's *thirty* pounds. Second, he's gorgeous. And third, I really do have to pee, so let's go."

In the bathroom Abby reapplied her lipstick as Maggie walked from the stall. "He's a hot one. He has that sort of rugged-but-looks-great-in-a-suit thing going on. I can't believe it."

"Thanks," Abby deadpanned.

"No. Not that I can't believe he's with you. I can't believe how good-looking he is. What's with the George Clooney gray temples? Are they real?"

"What are you *talking* about?"

"Some guys are dyeing their temples gray. It's very trendy."

"He's not dyeing them, trust me. He's embarrassed by them."

"Embarrassed? They're sexy. He's a hot one."

"You already said that."

"Damn it," Maggie said as she applied mascara. "You know what? It actually makes him sexier that the gray temples embarrass him. It's like a flaw he has no control over. Like he's vulnerable or something. Where'd you find this guy?"

Abby stopped adjusting her makeup and looked at her sister in the mirror. "You know I'm dating him, right? He's not some guy we just saw at the bar."

"Oh, give me a break! You know he's gorgeous. I'm just confirming it. Plus my hormones are crazy." Maggie lowered her voice to a whisper. "Do you know it's been four months since Jim and I've had sex?"

"Okay, we've already had this discussion. Can we *not* go there tonight?"

"I'm just telling you, if this baby doesn't come out soon, I don't know what I'm going to do. All my friends think something's wrong with me. None of them had any sex drive when they were this pregnant. But me? Watch out." Maggie was fanning herself with her hand.

"I'll make sure to keep Joel at a safe distance." Abby packed up her purse and headed for the bathroom door.

Maggie took one last look in the mirror. "Good idea."

They found the guys at the bar. Jim was still recovering from that year's Christmas glögg—a particularly nasty batch that left him with a headache he hadn't been able to shake for a week.

He raised his glass. "It's New Year's and I'm drinking Coke. All because he forced me to have a third glass of his glögg wine. One is too many, and two is insane. I don't know what I was thinking."

The women walked over. Joel put his arm around Abby. "Jim was just telling me about your father's glögg wine. I hear it's a family favorite."

"That's the one good thing about being this pregnant," Maggie said. "It got me out of the mandatory one-glass minimum."

They found their seats for dinner, and Maggie excused herself three times to use the restroom. At nine thirty the dance floor quickly filled. Maggie pulled Abby into the crowd, and they danced with the rest of the mob. When a slow song played, Joel and Jim joined them. They spent thirty minutes on the floor, then took a breather at the dinner table. Jim went for drinks.

"What time is it?" Maggie asked, out of breath.

"Almost ten thirty," Joel said.

"Hour and a half," she huffed. "I can make it."

She chugged water when Jim returned and then pulled Abby to the bathroom for the fifteenth time. She got her second wind at quarter past eleven, and all four headed back to the dance floor. The Electric Slide, and then a few oldies, assured that the floor was packed by quarter to twelve. Jim passed out hats, confetti, and horns. Waitresses served champagne. A few guests chewed on cigars and waited for midnight. The band fell silent. The lights dimmed and the crowd chanted.

Ten, nine, eight, seven, six, five, four, three, two, one. Happy New Year!

Bouncing among elbows and shoulders, Joel grabbed Abby by the waist. Balloons fell from overhead and the band started up again.

"Happy New Year," he said.

"Happy birthday," Abby replied.

Joel narrowed his eyes as his face broke into a smile. "You remembered?"

"Of course I remembered."

He pulled her close and kissed her. This time wasn't like the others. It wasn't a nervous kiss or hesitant. There were no second thoughts. It was purposeful, with Joel's hands on her hips, Abby's on his face. They were at the nucleus of two hundred people, mobbed by a mosh pit of drunken New Year's celebrators.

"Alright, already," Maggie said. "Get a room."

They broke apart. Maggie was right next to them, her hands on the small of her back, her belly screaming for them to get out of the way, and her face fire-engine red with strands of sweaty hair stuck to her cheek.

"This pregnant lady's gotta get home. My feet are killing me. They don't even fit into my flip-flops. Happy New Year." She hugged Abby. "Don't let this guy go," she whispered. She gave Joel a hug. "Happy New Year. Keep making my sister happy."

"I will," Joel said.

Abby and Joel waved as Jim limped Maggie off the dance floor and into the elevator. They stayed for another hour, then decided to pack it in. Joel helped Abby into the Range Rover and shut the door. Twenty minutes later they were in front of Abby's place.

"Thanks for inviting me," he said. "It was fun. The best New Year's I can remember. I'm usually on call, waiting to operate on some idiot who drove his car into a pole."

"That sounds like a terrible way to spend your birthday. Which reminds me, you've got to come in," Abby said. "I have to give you your present."

Inside, Joel turned down a drink and opted for coffee instead. Abby set him up with ingredients in the kitchen and excused herself to change. Her feet were aching. Joel hung his jacket over the back of the Pottery Barn chair and loosened his tie. When Abby walked down the stairs a few minutes later, the coffee machine was gurgling. She wore pink sweatpants and a Victoria's Secret tank top. She held a present in her hand.

"Happy birthday," she said as she walked into the kitchen.

Joel took the gift. "I don't know what to say. I'm surprised you remembered."

"Your birthday? Come on, how could I forget? A new year for the rest of us, a new decade for you?"

"Rub it in. Keep going."

She pointed to the present. "Open it."

They sat down at the table. Joel unwrapped the present and pulled out a tie. "Wow. I like it."

"It's a Domenico Vacca."

He raised his eyebrows. "Very nice. Very *Hollywood*."

"It'll look good on you."

He unknotted his tie and pulled it from his neck, then put together a haphazard half Windsor with the Domenico Vacca. "What do you think?"

Abby stood from her chair and walked over to him. She stood between his knees, reached down and adjusted the tie, tightening and straightening it and patting his collar down. "I was right, it looks nice on you."

He reached up and traced her lips with his finger. His hand ran across her face and then found the silky slope of her neck. They stared at each other while the coffee pot dripped. Abby slowly lowered herself until their lips met. Her weight was stored in her hands, which rested on his sturdy shoulders, and after a minute they kissed less gingerly. His hands floated to her waist and her heart surged when they touched the bare belt of skin where her shirt ended and the waistband of her sweats began. Abby leaned into him, and the chair creaked against the hardwood. His hands drifted north, under her shirt and along her back. They were warm and soft on her skin and filled her chest with electricity as her heart raced.

Her mind was racing too. She kissed harder, hoping to run off the intruding thoughts. She thought about Ben. About their secret study fortress at college. About their first kiss. About how she felt then and how she felt now. They were irrational considerations, but there was substance to them at the same time. Even this long after his death, she still felt connected to the first man she had ever loved. That connection was now pulling her away from the only other man she had loved in her lifetime.

Joel stood from the chair, stared at her for a second, and then kissed her again while he pulled her waist into his. Abby ran a hand through the back of his hair, and then down his shoulders as she backed against the kitchen counter. She wasn't sure what to do. She thought about gently pushing him away to regroup and collect her thoughts. But as confused as she was, she didn't want the moment to pass, and she didn't want to stop kissing him. She felt Joel's hands slide down to her hips. She placed her hands on the counter, and with Joel's help she lifted herself up until she was sitting on the granite. He moved closer, and without thinking Abby reached for the buttons of his shirt and began popping them open. As her hand ran over his smooth chest, she felt his hand slip between the skin of her waist and the band of her sweats.

Just then, Abby's phone rang. It startled both of them, and interrupted Abby's torrent of emotions. Joel slowly removed his hands from her waist as Abby looked at her watch. It was almost two in the morning. Her phone continued to sound.

Joel backed away, and Abby let herself off the kitchen counter. She picked up her phone and answered it.

"Hello?"

She looked at Joel.

"Oh God. I'll be right there."

Abby ended the call.

"Maggie's in labor. I've got to get to the hospital."

Chapter 44

Arrivals and Departures

Monday, January 1
8:03 p.m.

Ryan Alexander popped his head into the world on the night of New Year's Day. Abby's mother and father, as well as Jim's parents, roamed the hospital for the entire day while Maggie was in labor. As promised, Abby kept her mother at a safe distance and was present in the delivery room when Ryan Alexander was born. Jim was a mess—incoherent and unresponsive. He blamed it on the glögg wine from the week before.

At 8:03 p.m., the little guy made his appearance to his new family—four proud grandparents lined the window of the nursery and stared at the blue-bundled miracle who squirmed in the tiny crib. Abby had changed from the scrubs she'd worn in the delivery room back into her jeans and sweatshirt. She watched from the hallway as her parents fussed over Ryan, laughing when he slivered open a swollen eye. Her parents had done this once before, many years ago, and Abby had always wondered what they had looked like when they saw Jacob for the first time. Only Abby and Ben knew how dire Jacob's prognosis was back then; they hadn't immediately told their parents. The news was too much to process themselves, let alone explain to others. The memory brought tears, which Abby quickly blotted away. She didn't want to take attention away from Maggie and Jim and their brand new, healthy baby boy. Quietly, she ducked into the elevator.

She called Joel on the way home, but it was late, and she got no answer. She hadn't slept for a day and a half, and by the time the cab dropped her at her house, Abby was exhausted. It took her just seconds to fall asleep once her head hit the pillow.

It was 11:00 p.m. on New Year's Day. Joel had driven Abby to the hospital at two that morning after the phone call had interrupted them in the kitchen. He stayed for an hour before Abby told him to go home. Maggie was hysterical about Jim's fainting and worried about their mother's imminent arrival; Abby would have her hands full. Joel kissed Abby good-bye, made her promise to give him updates throughout the night, and then drove home. At noon, after a few hours of sleep, he headed to Journey Care to see his father.

It had been a particularly bad day, and his father's breathing was more labored than usual. Joel had feared he wouldn't make it through the afternoon. But he did, and into the night. Joel now sat next to his father's bed. He knew what was coming, and that if his father made it to the following day the hospice room would be filled with Joel's siblings and nieces and nephews gathering to say good-bye. This would likely be the last time Joel was alone with his father. He leaned close and whispered in his ear

"Dad. I'm sorry I never told you about what happened at the river. I'm sorry I didn't tell you that night, and I'm sorry I never told you afterward. I've spent my whole life beating myself up over it. I don't think I could have changed what happened. He'd still be gone, but maybe if I had told you, it would have changed my relationship with you. That's my biggest regret, that I let what happened at that damned river come between you and me. I watched how that secret hurt you over the years. I watched how it affected you and Mom and your relationship with me and Rachel and Brandon. I couldn't have changed what happened at the river that day, but I could have made things easier for you. I could have told you exactly what happened rather than allowing you to imagine it for yourself. Had I told you, Dad, I think things would have been different between us.

"Despite our tough times with each other, I want you to know that the man I am today is a reflection of you. It's taken me a long time to see that, but I'm proud of the person you turned me into. I'm proud to have you as my father."

Joel leaned even closer, so that his lips were nearly touching his father's ear. His eyes teared as he thought of his brother.

"Wherever he is now, I'm sure he's waiting for you, Dad."

"Dr. Keaton?"

Joel looked up to see the nurse in the doorway.

"I wanted to let you know that I'm leaving for the night. The night staff will take over. I told them what was happening with your dad, and they'll take good care of him."

"Thank you."

"You're welcome to stay as long as you'd like tonight."

"No," Joel said. "I'm getting ready to leave now. But I'll be back tomorrow. I'll bring my sister . . . just in case. I'll get ahold of my brother, too."

"That's a good idea. I'll be back in the morning," the nurse said.

"I'll see you then."

Chapter 45

The Letter

Tuesday, January 2
9:15 a.m.

At 9:15 a.m. on the morning of January 2, the woman pulled her car to the curb outside of Abby Gamble's home. It was a new year, and she was keeping the promise she had made to herself. She took the letter that sat on the passenger seat, one of many Ben had written to her during the course of their relationship, and read it one last time. So much had happened in such a short amount of time, she wanted to read Ben's words to remind herself that she was making the right decision.

She waited in her car for fifteen minutes, searching for the courage she would need. She'd struggled with this decision for more than a year. Finally she opened the car door, and, with Ben's letter in her hand, walked to the front of the house. She climbed the steps, raised her hand to the door, hesitated just a moment, and then knocked.

After leaving his father's bedside the night before, Joel had gone home to get a couple hours of sleep. Then he called

Abby for an update on Maggie. Abby had given him brief details on the phone, and then invited him over for coffee to give him the full story. She was planning to head back to the hospital soon, and Joel was set to meet his brother and sister at Journey Care in an hour. They each had a small window, and after the way New Year's had ended, they both wanted to see each other.

He pulled his Range Rover into a tight spot, left the engine running, and jogged into a coffee shop. He ordered a black coffee for himself and a cappuccino for Abby, plus two blueberry scones. He carried his order back to the car, placed everything in the back seat, and pulled from the curb on his way to Abby's house.

Abby heard the knock at the door. She was showered and dressed, and after a long night of sleep, felt rested and refreshed. Joel had offered to bring breakfast that morning. He wanted to hear everything about Maggie's delivery before Abby headed back to the hospital. She felt a bit of apprehension as she headed to the front door now. New Year's had ended so abruptly and awkwardly—with Abby sitting on the kitchen counter and Joel's shirt unbuttoned—that she wasn't sure how things would go when she saw him now.

She walked to the front door and pulled it open. But instead of Joel, a woman was standing on the front porch. A long, exhaled breath left the woman's lips in a white vapor that floated into the cold morning air. Abby recognized her as the woman who had mysteriously approached her weeks ago in front of her house before awkwardly running back to her car and driving off. Abby remembered the white envelope the woman had held in her hand that day and noticed that she was holding the same envelope now.

"Can I help you?"

The woman nodded. Her face was distressed. Abby

watched her take another deep breath, which left her body in the same white cloud of vapor.

"I need to talk to you about your husband."

"My husband?"

Abby stood in the foyer with the front door open and the cold morning air spilling into her house.

"Yes. I'm sorry to show up unannounced like this, but I really need to speak with you."

Abby pulled the front door all the way open and gestured for the woman to come inside, which she did.

"How do you know my husband?"

"That's what I want to talk with you about."

"Are you with the airline?" Abby asked as she slowly closed the door.

"The airline? No."

Abby cleared her throat. "My husband died last year."

The woman nodded. "Yes, I know. I apologize, I'm very nervous. I know Ben died, and I'm very sorry for your loss. But that's not why I'm here. Not exactly, anyway."

It sounded odd hearing Ben's name come from this woman's mouth.

"So what *is* this about?" Abby asked.

"I wrote a letter to you and your husband a couple of years ago."

"A letter?"

"Yes, it was an introduction letter. And a thank you."

"I'm not sure what you're talking about."

"Your husband never shared my letter with you, but he wrote back to me and agreed to meet."

Abby shook her head. "Ben agreed to meet you? About what?"

"About your son, Jacob."

Chapter 46

Waiting on a Heart

Tuesday, January 2
9:30 a.m.

The mention of Jacob's name caused Abby's knees to buckle. She had no chance of making it to the living room couch or into the kitchen. Instead, she simply lowered herself onto the stairs while the woman continued to talk.

"Ten years ago," the woman said, "my son was very sick. He was born with cardiomyopathy, a congenital heart condition that's usually fatal. His only chance was to undergo a heart transplant. As we put my son's name on the transplant list, the hardest part wasn't waiting for a heart, but knowing that the only way for our child to live was for someone else's to die. Hope for my child was tied directly to another parent's misery. I struggled with that for many years. Finally I wrote a letter to the parents of my son's donor and delivered it to the organ procurement organization. It was up to them to decide if they would pass my letter on to you and your husband. A few months later, I received a letter from Ben. He wanted to meet."

Abby shook her head, ran a trembling hand through her

hair. Her and Ben's decision to donate Jacob's organs had been for themselves as much as for anyone else. It was a way to assign meaning to Jacob's life and had been a therapeutic tool they each used to soften the blow of their son's death. Over the years, Abby had often thought of the recipients Jacob's organs might have helped.

"He never told me," Abby finally said. "About your letter. Ben never told me."

"I know. Ben was anxious to hear my story, and to hear about my child. But he was very worried, too."

"Worried about what?" Abby asked.

"About you. He explained to me that he wanted to find the best way to tell you. Ben and I met three times, and each time he talked about you. He told me everything you both went through. He told me that losing Jacob had nearly destroyed your marriage, and that it had taken a long time for you to reconstruct your life. He wanted to protect you, but he also wanted you to know that Jacob's death saved my son. He was very clear about that, about wanting you to know. And that's the only reason I'm telling you now. Ben was trying to find the best way to tell you about this."

The woman took a deep breath as her eyes teared up.

"Then, just before he planned to tell you, he got on that airplane."

The woman began to cry as she stood in Abby's foyer.

"I was left with the burden of telling you about Jacob and how his heart saved my son. I've put this day off for a year. It's been killing me not to tell you. Ben wanted you to know, but I haven't had the courage to tell you until now. I am so truly grateful to you and Ben. And to Jacob, as well."

Abby cried now, too. She stood from the stairs and the two women hugged each other. Strangers brought together by a bond so powerful they each felt it in the other's embrace.

"Thank you for telling me," Abby said.

Abby pushed the woman to arm's length and left her hands on the woman's shoulders.

"How is your son?" Abby asked.

The woman smiled. "He's perfect," she said through tears and a hoarse voice. "Perfect, and beautiful, and healthy. All because of Jacob. Ben met him, my son. I'd love for you to meet him, too."

Abby nodded. "I'd love that. More than you could ever imagine, I would love that."

Joel parked the Range Rover in front of Abby's house and climbed out. He grabbed the coffee and muffins from the back seat and walked up the snow-covered steps. He knocked on the front door. Abby answered a moment later. Her eyes were red-rimmed, and her cheeks were wet with tears.

"What's wrong?" Joel asked.

Abby shook her head. "Come on in. It's been a crazy morning."

Joel slowly walked through the doorway and into the foyer, worried about what was happening. Remembering how things had ended on New Year's Eve, he was troubled by the thought that Abby was about to tell him she was not ready for a relationship with him.

Joel stopped as soon as he saw the woman standing in the hallway.

"Rachel?" he said to his sister. "What are you doing here?"

PART V

GOING HOME

Chapter 47

Holding Hands

Tuesday, January 2
10:37 a.m.

Abby sat in her living room with Joel and Rachel. She had gathered her emotions, at least enough to brew Rachel a cup of coffee. Now, she sat next to Joel on the couch with Rachel across from her as they discussed and dissected the unimaginable and numinous links that tied all of their lives together. The fact that Abby and Joel were in a relationship was a shock to Rachel. That Abby had been married, and that her husband had died a year and a half ago, answered many questions for Joel. That Rachel and Ben had met to discuss the best way to tell Abby that Jacob's heart had been donated to Rachel's son, Brian, was a shock to all of them.

"I've actually met your son," Abby said.

"You've met Brian?" Rachel asked.

Abby nodded. "A couple of months ago. I went sledding with him and Joel."

Rachel shook her head. "I remember that. Brian told me about Uncle Joel's girlfriend, and that she was really nice."

Abby shook her head. "He's a sweet kid. He helped me with Joel's Christmas present."

"The Cubs convention?"

Abby smiled. "Yeah."

"Brian was online researching that for a full day," Rachel said. She looked at her brother. "So this is the woman who has you acting like a lovestruck teenager?"

Abby smiled. "Has he been acting strange?"

"Only for the last year. Having Brian over for sleepovers. Doing something other than work. Showing up Christmas morning in a Santa suit, which scared the hell out of my two-year-old."

"I'm outnumbered here," Joel said. "And there's all kinds of stuff happening right now, so I won't even try to fight back."

"He watched *Casablanca* the other night," Abby said.

"No!" Rachel's eyes were wide.

"Well, he fell asleep ten minutes into it, but he tried at least."

"See what I mean?" Rachel said. "I've never seen him watch anything other than baseball or football."

Abby smiled as she looked at Joel, patted his knee. "I've changed over the last year, too. This guy has a lot to do with it."

They talked for another hour in Abby's living room, deciding on the best way to tell Brian about Jacob. Brian had inquired over the years about his donor heart and how he had come to receive it.

Joel's phone buzzed and he checked the text message that came through. He held up his phone and looked at Rachel. "It's Brandon. He's at Journey Care with Dad and wondering where we are."

Rachel looked at her watch. "Wow. I've been here all morning. I thought I was going to stop for just a moment." She looked at Abby. "I'm sure Joel's told you about our father."

"He has," Abby said. "Go. We'll talk later and figure everything out."

"Come with us?" Rachel asked.

"Oh, I'm not sure that would be right."

"Yeah," Joel said. "Come with us."

Abby paused. "Are you sure?"

Joel nodded. "I'm sure. I'd love for him to meet you."

A few minutes later they walked out the front door on the way to see Joel's father. On the way down the front steps, Joel saw Rachel take Abby's hand.

Chapter 48

The Last Notch

Tuesday, January 2
10:00 p.m.

Ben and William dragged the boat to the water's edge. They had finished building it under the light of the moon, just the two of them working against time. And now, as silver moonlight floated on the ocean and reached the horizon, they stood on the beach and stared out into the night.

"That should do it," Ben said when they had the bow of the boat floating in the water.

"Yeah," William said. "You leave first thing in the morning?"

Ben nodded. "That's the plan."

"Do you have everything you need?"

"I do."

"After you make it . . . come back and find us."

"I will. You'll be okay?"

The kid smiled. "We'll be fine."

Knowing their time together was coming to an end, they both stared at each other.

"Thanks for everything you've done for us," William said.

"I've still got one last thing to do. Just to make sure."

William nodded. "I really appreciate it."

"You got me this far," Ben said. "And a promise is a promise." Ben stuck out his hand and the kid shook it. "I'll see you in the morning. I won't leave without saying good-bye."

Ben walked away from the kid and the boat they'd built. Then he turned and headed up the beach. He walked past the partially submerged nose of the downed plane, beyond his shack, and into the forest. When he reached the red cedar, he unfolded his Swiss Army knife and carved one final notch into the trunk. He stood up and looked at his handiwork and the hundreds of lines etched into the tree. This was the last one he'd carve.

Chapter 49

A Better Place

Tuesday, January 2
11:54 p.m.

Perhaps if his father had passed sooner, just after he'd grown ill, it would have been easier. But it would have been more tragic, too. Something had happened during the months his father was on his deathbed. Joel had confessed his sins, had gotten his secret off his chest, and in some strange way felt closer to his father now than ever in the past. When Joel brought Abby to the bedside and introduced her, his father managed to squint an eye open. It was enough to confirm that his father knew his son was happy.

The Keaton kids stayed by his bedside until late into the evening. Their father hung on, refusing to let go. Finally, approaching midnight, they decided to leave and return in the morning. After Joel dropped Abby at her house, he headed home. When he climbed into bed, it didn't take long before he was dreaming. So much was going on in his mind. He found himself in his childhood home, looking for the deer through the window of his father's study. He had the urge to jump from the couch and run to the river to convince his brother not to venture out across the log. But this time something kept him on the couch. Thoughts of his brother faded. The brush moved at the edge of the woods, and then he saw it. A large doe stepped through the foliage and sprang effortlessly into the openness of the backyard. It was hypnotic how the animal merged with the forest like a chameleon. She was nearly invisible despite being only yards away. As hard as the doe was to spot, once Joel had her in his sights, everything else disappeared.

He stared without moving, watching the deer as it stayed as still as he. He saw the caramel-colored eyes, the scar that ran along her chest near her heart, and he knew it was the same deer he'd seen before. The tranquility of the moment was offset by the stranger Joel had come to know in his dreams, who walked from the woods only ten yards from the deer. Miraculously, the animal did not run. The man waved for Joel to join him. Joel was hesitant, worried that a startled movement by him would send the deer into a sprint. He slowly slipped off the couch, opening the screen door with equal stealth. When he placed a foot carefully onto the grass, the deer looked at him but otherwise stayed still. Joel paused for several seconds, only a few feet from the animal.

"It's okay," the man said. "She won't run."

Joel crept closer. The man walked next to the deer and nodded for Joel to join him.

"I don't want to scare her," Joel whispered.

"She's not scared," the man said. "Not anymore."

Joel approached, amazed at the bulk of her shoulders. Her body was smooth and muscular, individual striations visible through the fawn coating. He lifted his trembling hand and ran his palm along the length of her back. Her coat was like silk, her body warm.

"She's beautiful," Joel said.

"Gorgeous."

Both men stared at the doe and a long time passed before either spoke. Finally the man looked at Joel. "It's not your fault."

Joel stared but said nothing.

"The day at the river. It's not your fault."

Joel squinted his eyes, unsure how to react to his secret pouring from the stranger in front of him.

"You couldn't have saved him. And preventing yourself from happiness now won't bring him back. You weren't a doctor thirty years ago at that river. You didn't have the same abilities to help people that you have today. You were a scared ten-year-old kid. And maybe, because of your brother and that river, you're able to help people today in ways that are foreign to most."

Joel looked into the animal's eyes as he contemplated the man's words.

"We all want an extra day with the people we love most," the man said. "It's natural. One more day to tell them all the things we wished we had told them when we had the chance. Oftentimes, we believe that extra day isn't available to us. But it is. If we pay attention to what's important, it is. If we take advantage of our time, it is. If we're aware of what we have, that extra day is right in front of us."

The man placed his hand on the deer's back.

"She trusts you now. It wasn't easy; she's been hurt in the past. But now she knows."

Joel looked away from the animal's eyes and at the man next to him. "Knows what?"

"She knows you'll never hurt her," he said. "And so do I. She's all yours. Take good care of her."

The man backed away from Joel and the deer and disappeared into the forest.

A faraway noise caught Joel's attention. It was a ringing sound that came from inside his childhood home. He looked again at the doe, ran his hand along her back one more time, and then hurried across the lawn and through the screen door. In his father's study, the ringing grew louder until he realized the noise was coming from the phone positioned on his father's desk. He slowly reached for it, picked it up, and placed it to his ear.

After another second, it rang again. And again. And again.

Joel opened his eyes. His bedroom was dark besides the glowing of his cell phone on his nightstand. The phone was ringing, and he finally came back from his dream. He sat up and stared at the caller ID. It was the hospice facility.

"Hello?"

"Dr. Keaton. This is Nancy from Journey Care. I'm afraid your father has passed."

It took him a moment to understand, and then another to clear his throat before he answered her. "Okay. I'll be right over."

As he ended the call, he waited for sadness to hit him. He waited, but it never came. Instead, Joel felt peace. A clairvoyant sensation that told him his father was in a better place and was no longer suffering. Perhaps, Joel imagined, his father was in a place where he would see his son again after so many years without him.

Chapter 50

The Arrival

Wednesday, January 3
11:18 a.m.

Christian Malone's corporate jet flew nonstop from San Francisco to Tahiti. They had left on January 2 at 3:00 p.m., and Christian spent the eight-and-a-half-hour flight entertaining his investors. They arrived at Fa'a'ā International Airport in Tahiti and spent the night at a hotel Christian had arranged. The following morning, on January 3, the group boarded two floatplanes that would take them on the final leg of their journey—another hour into a remote part of the South Pacific, where land was nowhere in sight and only the blue, wide-open ocean stretched to the horizon. Then, as the floatplane began its descent, Valhalla Island came into view—a tiny patch of land in the middle of the vast blue ocean.

Christian pressed his forehead against the plane's window like a child on his first flight. The water landing was tricky. The approach had to be made on the eastern side of the island, away from the fierce winds on the west end. The lure of this place was the kitesurfing opportunities it offered, but the high winds that made the sport so popular were not conducive to resort life. Sitting poolside, or lying on the beach, was not possible with furious winds blowing off the ocean. So the plan was to build the resort on the calm eastward side of the island and transport guests in a fleet of Humvees through the interior rain forest. Today, though, they'd make the trek on foot. They would tour the proposed location of the resort where Christian had, three years before, begun depositing building material and constructing temporary housing for the construction crews before Hurricane Earl halted production, caused an evacuation of the workforce, and wiped out nearly every shack they built.

The plane skimmed along the ocean and eventually touched down in a smooth landing. They glided on the water for thirty seconds before coming to a stop and floating on the surface with waves bobbing the plane up and down. The pilot unhooked himself from the cockpit, opened the side door, and climbed out and onto one of the large pontoons. He deployed a raft, which automatically inflated. Christian and his team exited the plane, boarded the raft, and quickly covered the hundred yards between the floatplane and the shore. When the bow of the raft met the soft sand of the island, Christian climbed onto the beach and spread his arms.

"Welcome to Valhalla Island, the site of one of the most exclusive resorts in the world. A place where extreme kite-surfers from around the globe will flock for a once in a lifetime experience."

After helping everyone onto dry land, Christian Malone turned from the ocean and walked up the beach toward the lagoon in the distance.

Chapter 51

The Picture

Wednesday, January 3
11:22 a.m.

Joel knocked on Abby's door ten minutes after he left Journey Care. She opened the door and immediately hugged him.

"I'm so sorry about your dad," she whispered in his ear.

He took her in his arms as they stood on the front porch.

"He got to meet you yesterday," Joel said. "That was really important to me."

"To me, too," Abby said. "Come on in. I'll be ready in a minute. There's coffee in the kitchen."

Joel walked inside and closed the front door while Abby disappeared up the stairs. Joel had called Rachel and Brandon after his middle-of-the-night notification from Journey Care. Together the Keaton siblings had gone to the hospice facility to say a final good-bye to their father, complete paperwork, and organize funeral plans. When they were finished, Joel's next call had been to Abby. She offered to take him to breakfast, and he accepted.

As he sipped coffee now and waited for Abby, Joel wandered the first floor. He admired the Christmas tree in the living room, remembering his and Abby's time together on Christmas Eve, which seemed like months ago despite barely being a week. He turned his attention to the mantel, where several framed photos sat. He removed each of them one by one and studied the people captured in them. Abby and Maggie. Abby and her parents. Jim and Maggie. A few older folks he took for grandparents. He saw the picture he had given Abby on Christmas Eve, from the toboggan slides, and smiled. He loved the way they looked together.

He stopped at the next picture. It caught his eye and drew him in. He lifted it from the mantel and stared. Framed in it were two men, father and son, it appeared. Both were holding fish in their outstretched arms and smiling broadly. The older gentleman was unfamiliar, but the younger man brought a sense of déjà vu, overwhelming him to the point that the room began to spin. Joel knew this man. He was younger in the picture, but the familiarity was unmistakable. He couldn't quite make the connection or determine his relationship to the man. As he stared at the picture, the distant affiliation faded in and out. He almost grasped it one moment, lost it the next.

Joel scrutinized the photo. The men were sitting in a boat near shore, and in the background was a dense forest. Joel's eyes widened when he figured it out. Like a forgotten thought resurfacing after a struggle to recall it, Joel's subconscious pulled the man's identity from the recesses of his mind. Joel remembered his childhood house. The bay window in his father's den. The forest. He remembered the deer. And finally, his thoughts settled on the stranger from his dreams—the man who had made an appearance in the recurrent dream Joel had had for the past many weeks. He looked harder at the person in the picture. He was sure.

It was the same man.

Abby looked into the bathroom mirror at her swollen eyes, congested and red from so much crying over the last two days. She took a deep breath and slowly exhaled.

"Get yourself together, girl," she whispered to her reflection.

So much had transpired over the last two days, starting with the birth of her nephew and seeing the joy it brought Maggie and her parents. Then Rachel's arrival on her doorstep and the information she offered, from discovering where Jacob's heart had gone—something she had secretly wondered about for years—to hearing that Ben had struggled with the proper way to tell her, to learning that he had died just before he planned to let her know. The emotional forty-eight hours had culminated with Joel's phone call this morning telling her that his father had passed. The tears seemed to be ever present now.

She took a moment to compose herself, then applied a light coat of concealer under her eyes, brushed her teeth, and shut off the bathroom light. She walked down the stairs and saw Joel standing in front of the fireplace.

"Ready?" she asked.

Joel turned from the mantel, an awkward smile on his face. "I was just looking at your pictures." He held up one of the photos. "Is this a picture of your . . . of Ben?"

Abby walked over and saw the picture of Ben and his father. It was the only one she had kept; the others had been stashed months ago. Tears welled in her eyes again as her two worlds collided, old and new. She forced a smile and nodded. "Yeah, that's Ben." The tears spilled down her face, and she wiped her cheeks. "I was going to move it . . ." She shrugged, "I just never did."

She watched as Joel looked back at the picture. He stared

at it for a moment longer, smiling, Abby noticed, as if he were looking at the photo of an old and dear friend. Then he leaned over and kissed her on the forehead.

"Don't move it," he said. "It belongs right here."

Joel placed the photo of Ben next to the one of him and Abby.

Chapter 52

The Discovery

Wednesday, January 3
11:25 a.m.

Everyone climbed from the raft and headed across the beach. Although it had been more than two years since he stepped foot on this island, Christian recognized the land. He led the group of investors up the beach and toward the lagoon. But before they made it far, he stopped suddenly and held out his arms for everyone else to do the same. To go no farther. Up ahead, he noticed a wide path of destruction. Toppled palm trees slanted inland. The ground held deep gouges as if a massive clearing machine had taken a single pass through the area but had never gone back a second time.

The investors stayed on the beach as Christian continued walking. Cautiously, he headed farther inland until it materialized before him. He recognized what he was looking at but could hardly admit it to himself. A Transcontinental Airlines flight had gone missing a couple of years earlier. Although widely believed to have crashed into the Pacific Ocean, the fuselage had never been found. Christian Malone was sure he was looking at it now. The nose of the plane was sunk beneath the surface of a lagoon, and the massive hulk of metal he was looking at had been torn away from the rest of the plane. He looked around, as far as his eyesight allowed, but the rest of the plane was nowhere to be seen. Was this tiny postcard of an island where the crew had tried to land the doomed plane?

The destructive path of fallen palms trees, however, told another story. Christian imagined that the pilots must have attempted a water landing. The plane, though, had been ripped to pieces in the process. The nose must have skimmed across the ocean and onto shore, destroying everything in its path until it came to rest here in this lagoon, just feet from where he had planned to build his resort. As he stared at the wreckage, a thought descended upon him. Could anyone have survived this tragedy?

Christian walked along the edge of the lagoon and approached the massive fragment of the 747. The destruction was terrifying, with the metal torn cleanly in some areas, jaggedly ripped away in others. He approached the wreckage and got a good look inside the cabin. Some seats were still intact in the first-class section, but many were missing. He looked into the rain forest and his gaze fell on the shacks his construction crew had built years earlier. Three were left standing; the others were no more than piles of rubble.

He slowly walked toward the shacks, leaving the wreckage behind. He took a quick look back to the beach and saw his investors standing where he'd left them, quizzical looks of bewilderment on their faces. Christian motioned for them to stay put. For the moment, the island belonged to Christian and it was his job to investigate the scene they had stumbled upon. He turned and headed toward the first shack. When he reached it, he pushed open the door and found it empty. He slowly turned his head to the second shack, jogged over, and pushed open the door. Empty. There was only one shack left, and he headed for it, his feet sinking into the sand as he walked. Finally he reached the structure. Slowly, he pushed the door open and peered inside. All three shacks were empty, with no sign of life.

He looked around one more time, settled his gaze on the nose of Flight 1641, pulled out his satellite phone and dialed.

Chapter 53

A Promise Kept

Wednesday, January 3
11:25 a.m.

Ben stood at the edge of the lagoon with William at his side. Off to his right was the front half of the plane with its nose sunk beneath the surface. As Ben stared at his reflection he tried to make out his eyes, but subtle waves distorted his features and jetted his reflection in up-and-down ripples.

"I know you're anxious to get going," William said. "I know you're ready to get back to your wife."

Ben tried to work through his emotions. There was an ache deep in his heart that caused him to shiver when he imagined an existence without Abby. A hush fell over the island, and as Ben continued to stare at the surface of the lagoon, his reflection flattened. The tiny waves and ripples that distorted his image passed, and for an instant he saw his own eyes clearly on the surface of the water. He knew which route he had to take, and in which direction to head. He finally understood the path that would take him back to her. All at once, it was obvious to him.

A crash interrupted his thoughts as William dove into the

water and swam with powerful strokes to the middle of the lagoon.

"Come on," William yelled to Ben. "I need to show you something."

The kid took on an effortless backstroke as he headed to the other side of the lagoon. Ben hesitated for a moment, and then dove in. He knifed beneath the surface and allowed his momentum to push him deep under water. A sense of peace and tranquility came over him as he speared into the crystal blue water. After a few strokes and kicks that brought him deeper into the lagoon, he stopped swimming and found himself neutrally buoyant, sitting suspended deep below the water's surface. Visibility was endless, and as he turned and pulled himself horizontally through the water, he noticed how quiet it was. His lungs didn't ache, he had no urge for breath, and he felt as though he could stay there for an eternity.

He finally looked above him to see the surface dancing with the sun's rays. He headed upwards, releasing the air from his lungs as he rose, and broke through the surface into the morning sunlight. He floated on his back and took on an easy drift while William swam next to him. They each allowed the current to carry them, and before long the airplane wreckage was a small thing on the other side of the lagoon.

"Keep your legs up," William said. "And your feet out in front of you."

Ben turned his attention from the faraway airplane and noticed the lagoon pouring into narrows that led to the river. The current grew stronger as the water bottlenecked into the channel. Ben positioned himself as William suggested—in a sitting position with his feet in front of him. The current swept them both into the river where they rode on the shoulders of the stream. In front of them Ben saw a tree that had fallen across the narrow river and two rocks that protruded high into the air. The water splashed around the stones and swirled in tiny eddy currents.

In one swift motion, William met the felled log and pulled himself onto it, helping Ben do the same. They sat on the log and watched the river rage beneath them. Ben felt as though the surroundings did not belong to him, as if he were in someone else's domain and should not touch or disturb anything.

Long shadows lay across the river and William pointed to them. "See those shadows?"

Ben nodded.

"That's how I learned my sense of direction, based on which way the sun was slanting the shadows of the trees. My dad taught my brothers and me that the shadows point to the west in the morning, east in the evening."

Ben kept his eyes on the shadows, understanding that something greater was transpiring here.

"This is where it happened," William said. "Where my life ended. I used to be scared to come here. When I first arrived, the river frightened me. But now, I feel at home here."

He pointed to the rocks in front of them.

"I fell from that rock when I was sixteen years old, and the river sucked me away. My younger brother watched the whole thing, and for a long time I felt terrible that I put him through it. He's carried that burden with him his entire life, and I haven't been able to help him get past it. But then you showed up, and I understood how it was supposed to work. Your journey was meant to go through my brother. You helped him finally understand that my death was not his fault."

The kid stood on the log and looked at Ben. "You did it by letting go of your wife and allowing her to fall in love. Abby changed my brother's life. Without her love, Joel would have stayed stuck in the past. I know that wasn't easy for you— letting Abby go. Thanks for keeping your promise." William smiled. "I'm finally free."

Ben thought of Abby while he sat on the log as the river

thundered below him. Taking that final step—allowing Abby to drift into the arms of another man—was like jumping off a thousand-foot high dive. But he knew it was the only way for their story to end. Then Ben thought of his son. Over the years, Jacob had been his closest companion. As he sat above the raging river in this final leg of his journey, Ben's heart ached, and he understood why. His journey from life to death had brought him to this crossroads—in one direction was his wife. In the other, his son.

William jumped off the log and into the river, allowing the current to take him.

"What are you doing?" Ben yelled.

The kid turned to face Ben as the river pulled him away "I'm going to go see my dad. He's finally here. You should go see Abby. It's time."

Chapter 54

The Staircase

Wednesday, January 3
11:25 a.m.

Ben watched William float down the river until he disappeared. Then he walked along the fallen log, jumped onto the riverbank, and headed into the forest. He knew where he needed to go. There was no more doubt. There was no more uncertainty. He finally knew exactly where he was headed. He walked for a long time before he found it, then stopped and stared upward. He always knew he'd end up here. He'd been searching for this place ever since his voyage from life to death had started. There was a part of him that wished he had arrived sooner. But a different part, the wiser part, understood that this transformation took time, and the winding path that had led him to this place was one he needed to follow. It was the path that led beyond his regrets and failures, to a world where redemption was an arm's length away and forgiveness hung thick in the air. It was a path that led to his dreams. The path of second chances.

Ben started up the staircase in front of him. His first step caused them to creak with a noise that took him back over the years, across time until, when he reached the top, he found himself at the forefront of a different life. It was there that he found her. Finally, after so long, he had found his way back to her—if only for a fleeting moment. When he saw her, he realized that his journey to this place had been paced just right. Had he gotten there any sooner, he would have done so without the ability to understand what was about to transpire. Any later, and he might not have reached it at all.

Chapter 55

The Fortress

Wednesday, January 3
10:02 p.m.

The New Year had ushered in a whirlwind of emotions. Nervous anticipation as Abby prepared to spend New Year's Eve with Joel. Passion and urges when she kissed him in her kitchen. Panic when she wanted things to go further, and relief when the opportunity was taken from her by Maggie's labor. Joy when she witnessed Maggie give birth. Sorrow when she relived her own journey to parenthood. Disbelief when Rachel showed up on her doorstep to tell her that her son had received Jacob's heart. Shock when she realized that boy was Brian. Clairvoyance when she appreciated how their lives were connected. Peace when she understood that it was all meant to be. Freedom when she told Joel everything about her past. Pain when she conjured up the details of losing Ben. Resolve when she decided to finally move forward. And happiness when she knew Joel would be part of her future.

When she laid her head on the pillow that night, she fell into a sound sleep that she had not known since anguish had infected her life the night Ben died. The deep slumber took her across the years. She allowed it to transform her. She climbed the stairs of their study fortress from college. She climbed them knowing what she would find. She climbed them with an ache in her heart. The old wooden staircase creaked under her feet, like it had the first time she climbed it, when she walked up these stairs and met the man of her dreams.

She was dreaming deeply as she pushed open the door to her past and took in the surroundings. Abby saw the desk in front of the half-moon window, and the pair of chairs positioned close to one another like old friends. The ancient exercise equipment stacked in the corner. As she walked into the room and approached the desk, thoughts of her time in this place rolled back to her like high tide—white-capped waves filled with memories of sleepless nights, endless talks with the man she loved, times of passion, and short stretches where the rest of the world disappeared. She walked to the desk and ran her hand over the surface.

"I thought you might be here."

Her eyes stopped moving, her lungs quit expanding, her mind stopped functioning, and all she concentrated on was the voice behind her. She couldn't move. Wouldn't allow herself to turn around for fear that her mind would realize she was dreaming, and he'd be gone. Those dreams had stopped a few months back. Perhaps their absence was a defense mechanism, a subconscious effort to end the torment. But when Abby heard his voice now, it felt genuine. Different from those old dreams where she *wanted* it to feel real, where she tricked herself into believing that he was there in front of her. This time was not like the others. His voice was reassuring and comforting and held within it a remedy to heal old wounds. Abby knew this was something more than a dream.

"I fell in love with you the first time I saw you," he said. "When you walked up these steps all those years ago, you stepped into my heart. You allowed me to step into yours, as well. I grabbed it and told you I'd never let go. I told you I'd love you forever."

Abby finally turned from the table. She blinked when she saw him framed in the doorway.

"Ben?"

She walked toward him and placed her hand on his face, feeling him for the first time in forever. His cheek was warm and soft, and covered by a subtle tingle of stubble.

"I'm giving it back to you now," he said. "I've held on to your heart long enough."

"But I still love you," Abby said.

"We'll always love each other. Forever, just like I promised you. For us, though, our love was meant to change. There's something else for you. Someone else you're meant to love. Someone who can give you all the things I never could."

"You gave me everything I ever wanted."

"No I didn't. And I came here to tell you I'm sorry."

"Ben." Her voice cracked as they stared at each other. "It's not your fault."

"I could have done more for you, Abby. I want to do it now. I want to give you what I couldn't before."

Abby cried.

"Do you love him?" Ben asked.

Abby looked to the ground, still with her hand on his face. She closed her eyes. "Yes."

Ben smiled. "Good. I did it."

Abby looked up at him. "Did what?"

He reached to his face and took her wrist, pushed her hand until it was over her own chest. "I gave you your heart back. I'll always be in there, but it belongs to someone else now."

Ben slowly backed away from her.

"I miss you," Abby said.

"I miss you, too. But you have so much happiness in your

274 *Brian Charles*

future. Joel's waiting for you. You're meant to spend your life with him."

"What about you?"

"There's someone else waiting for me."

A smile found her face. She ran the back of her hand across her cheek. "Will you get to see him?"

"I wouldn't call it heaven otherwise."

Abby worked hard not to cry. "Tell him I miss him."

"I will."

"And give him a kiss for me."

"It'll be the first thing I do."

Ben took a step back, until he was out of the doorway and on the landing of the stairs. Then he turned and was gone.

TWO MONTHS LATER

Chapter 56

The Package

Saturday, March 9
2:32 p.m.

Christian Malone sat in the Admiral's Club at San Francisco International Airport. He went back to the list he'd compiled. He was sure he had the correct name and address. It had been a two-month journey to get to this point. Despite an army of assistants, he'd done the research on his own, never asking for anyone's help. The airline had no idea that he had taken the item from the wreckage site, and never for an instant had Christian considered telling them about it. They'd have alerted NTSB, who would have secured it for further analysis and might never have delivered it to the right place. He'd found it washed up on shore the morning he had discovered Flight 1641, and when he saw the contents, he knew what he needed to do.

He watched the clock for twenty minutes, until it was time to board, then he picked up his small carry-on bag and left the lounge. He was seated comfortably in first class a few minutes later, and by the time he finished his soda the plane was racing down the tarmac. He closed his eyes and tried to sleep, but the four-hour flight dragged on. He had no interest in watching movies, and his concentration was not focused enough to read. So he stared out the window for the entirety of the flight and was grateful when the plane started its descent into Chicago O'Hare.

He had arranged transportation and found his driver outside baggage claim, holding a sign with his name. The driver offered to store Christian's lone bag in the trunk, but he refused. Instead he placed it on the seat next to him when he climbed into the Lincoln Town Car. He handed the driver the address and sat back as the car pulled into traffic.

Christian had not called ahead. Had not set up a formal meeting. He was here on his own journey. It was something he was called to do. If it worked out today, perfect. If not, he'd find a hotel and try again tomorrow. Or the next day, and for as many days as it took to deliver the package.

It took forty minutes through traffic before the driver turned onto the side street and surveyed the addresses. Two blocks later, they arrived.

"Wait for you?" the driver asked.

"Yeah. I'll be right back."

Christian opened the door, grabbed his carry-on bag from the seat next to him, and climbed out of the car. He pulled his jacket tight against the cold, walked over the dirty mound of snow that remained from winter, and up the steps to the home. He knocked on the front door. A woman answered a moment later and Christian Malone knew he was meant to be there. He was meant to hand over this parcel that had made the long journey from the South Pacific.

"Mrs. Gamble?"

"Yes?"

"My name is Christian Malone. I'm . . . I'm the one who discovered Flight 1641."

The woman nodded; her forehead wrinkled. "I've seen you on the news."

"I'm sorry to show up unannounced like this. But I had to find you."

He saw her squint slightly.

"Why?"

Christian placed his carry-on bag on the ground and unzipped it. Inside was the backpack he'd found on the island next to the wreckage of the plane. It had washed up on shore, he figured, and had come to rest on a lattice of bamboo that had prevented the surf from recapturing it and taking it back out to sea. Inside the backpack he had found a journal with Abby's name in it.

It had taken a few weeks for Christian to complete his research. He'd obtained the full passenger list of Flight 1641 but found no Abbys or Abigails on it. After some digging, though, he discovered that a passenger named Ben Gamble had a wife named Abigail. She owned a large cosmetics company. It didn't take much to find her address.

Christian was adamant about locating her because he had read just enough from the pages of the journal to know that this was a cherished diary of letters her husband had written to their son. It was something Christian had to return.

He pulled the backpack from his bag and handed it to Abby Gamble.

"I found this near the plane. There's a journal inside. I believe it belonged to your husband."

She reached into the backpack and pulled out Ben's hardcover journal. It was damaged by seawater and the pages were bloated and stiff. But as she quickly thumbed through it, she saw that nearly every page was legible.

Christian noticed the woman's hands begin to shake. When she looked up at him, she was crying.

"Thank you," she said before engulfing him in a tight hug.

THREE YEARS LATER . . .

Chapter 57

A Rocking Horse

Friday, August 3
1:22 p.m.

Joel walked the long corridor of the hospital and stopped at room 258. He pushed the heavy door open and entered. Abby sat up in the hospital bed and Joel walked over.

"How is she?"

Abby looked down at her sleeping daughter, bundled in blankets in her arms. "Perfect. She just ate, and now she's sound asleep."

Joel kissed his wife and ran his thumb over his daughter's silky cheek. "She's so beautiful."

Joel shook his head while he stared, bringing his forehead forward until it rested against Abby's. He kissed her again.

"I've got something for you." He placed a small package on the bed.

"What is it?"

"A present."

"A push present?"

"Not really. Just open it."

Abby kept one hand around her daughter and peeled away

the paper with the other. She removed the top of the thin box, and then the tissue paper. Her eyes teared when she looked inside the box. Her hand quivered, unable to lift the present from the felt in which it was seated.

"It's supposed to make you smile, not cry," Joel said.

Abby shook her head. "I'm not upset, it's wonderful."

She finally pulled from the box a gold-plated rocking horse ornament, "Amanda" engraved in cursive letters across the saddle.

"To match Jacob's," Joel said. "I ran it past your mom, and she gave me the okay to continue the tradition."

Abby stared at the ornament, and then looked at Joel. "I love you."

Joel kissed her. "I love you, too."

"Forever?" Abby asked before she knew the words were in her head or past her lips.

Joel smiled and looked from his daughter to his wife, then shook his head. "No. Longer than forever. Someone told me that I should always look for one extra day with the people I love the most. So it'll be forever, plus two days. One for each of you."

One week after she left the hospital, Abby gave Maggie her first babysitting assignment. It would only be for an hour, two at the most. She kissed Amanda, and ten minutes later walked into the Garden Club for lunch. She hadn't done this for years and hated herself for letting it get that far. Letting things go untouched for so long. She sat down and ordered water with lemon. She waited.

A few moments later Abby spotted her. She stood and waved. It was different this time around. Unrecognizable from the last. Abby no longer needed to run from her memories. When Ben's mother approached, they hugged like a long-lost mother-daughter combo. In a way, they were. Abby cried during the embrace. Ben's mother did the same.

"I'm sorry we haven't talked for so long," Abby said.

"I'm sorry, too, sweetie."

"I'm better now, and I have a lot to tell you about."

Ben's mother broke free from the embrace.

"Let me see her first."

Abby smiled and reached into her purse for pictures.

Epilogue

He sits across from me now as the boat rocks in a gentle swirl. We've become the type of friends I always imagined we'd be, and fishing is our grandest pastime. Something I loved to do with my own father on those early Saturday mornings and have learned to love again. But there's something different now. My son adds to it in a way that's difficult to explain, and perhaps can only be understood by a parent who has reconnected with a child they lost.

It's almost as though he was never gone; that our time apart was a mere blink. Magical things like that happen in the place we call heaven. A place with no illness or pain, and where everything is possible. He has an easy way about him, no worries, and every time I look at him I see his mother. I see Abby's eyes when he looks at me, and I see her smile when he laughs. I still think of Abby often, but I smile when I see her now; I'm looking through different eyes. She is safe, and her heart is no longer in danger. She has Joel and Amanda, and when I look down on them now, I can't help but feel lucky. In heaven I have it all. I'm truly blessed. I get to see her always and watch her joy. And I get to do it all with my son. He is such a part of me now that my old life looks distant and small from where I am.

The sun is rising, brimming over the horizon and spilling enchanted colors across the water. The moments of wonder my father introduced to me as a child are now shared with my son. Jacob sits across from me in the boat I built for this exact moment, his fingers in a concentrated motion as he ties his lure. He's perfected the Palomar knot that my father taught me, and I feel proud when I watch him. I see his lips move as he silently whispers words passed down through three generations.

Over, under, and through the loop.

Author's Note

A common question asked of authors is where the ideas for their stories come from. In the case of *Before I Go*, the inspiration came from a dream.

My mom passed away the year after I graduated from college. She was just fifty-two years old. Lung cancer had gone undetected until it spread to most of her body, including her brain. She suffered a stroke that robbed her of the ability to speak, and left her without the use of the right side of her body. Wheelchair-bound and bedridden, my mother's time in hospice was a difficult few weeks for my siblings and me. It was especially tough on our grandfather, who helplessly watched as his daughter faded away.

A strange thing happened, though, after my mom died. I was upset and sad, as would be expected. I was twenty-two years old and my mother's passing was my first experience with death. I didn't know what mourning was supposed to look or feel like, and I had no idea how long it was supposed to last. I would, however, quickly learn. Two weeks after my mom's passing, I had a vivid dream about her. I remember the dream today as clearly as if just waking from it. It happened while I was staying at my then-girlfriend's* parents' house. In the dream, my mother came to me and told me one thing: *I'm okay.*

Those were her exact words. *I'm okay.* When I woke, the sadness I had felt during the previous two weeks was gone. I knew my mom was in a better place. Somewhere with no illness or disease. A place where her ability to speak was restored, and where she was no longer confined to a wheel-chair. A place where she could walk and run and dance. I woke with a peaceful feeling in my heart that told me I no longer needed to worry about Mom. She was doing just fine.

In the twenty-plus years since I experienced that dream, I've lost others who were close to me. Grandparents, a beloved great-aunt, and a dear family friend. I have had equally vivid dreams about each of these people, all of them telling me one simple thing—that they were "okay." It seems my mom started a trend.

So when I sat down to write *Before I Go*, a story of love and loss and the powerful ways in which our lives are forever tied to the loved ones who pass before us, I did so with those dreams in mind and those loved ones in my heart. I hope this story touched you in some special way, and that you loved reading it as much as I loved writing it.

Brian Charles
February 2022

*P.S. That young woman I was dating when I had the dream about my mom . . . she's now my wife of twenty-plus years, and much of our love story is present in some fashion in the love Abby finds in the novel.

Acknowledgments

My sincere gratitude goes to the many people who helped make this novel possible:

Thanks to my agent, Marlene Stringer. This was the book that started our journey together. Thanks for never giving up on it.

Thanks to my editor, John Scognamiglio, for your suggestions that made this story more than it was when I sent it to you. And for the honor of publishing this novel under your imprint.

Thanks to my wife, Amy, for more than a quarter century of marriage, and for our love story that—like Ben and Abby's—started in college. I tried hard to do it justice in the pages of this novel.

Thanks to Abby Marie and Nolan Matthew—Abby, I started this book when you were an infant sleeping in a rocker next to me during early morning writing sessions. Nolan, you hadn't been born. Now teenagers, you both make me proud every day. The great blessing of being your dad inspired the love Abby and Ben share for their child.

Thanks to my friend, Capt. Rich Hills, for sharing your knowledge of aviation with me. It turns out that crashing a plane into the Pacific Ocean is quite challenging, and being unable to locate it for so long is even more so. Thanks, Rich, for giving me the tools to make it sound legit.

And finally, thanks Mom, for letting me know that you are A-Okay.

BEFORE I GO

ABOUT THIS GUIDE

The suggested questions are included to enhance
your group's reading of Brian Charles's
Before I Go!

Discussion Questions

1. *Before I Go* is a love story with a twist. What aspect of the story appealed to you that made you initially want to read it?

2. Making characters realistically fall in love in the confines of 300 pages is challenging. Was Abby and Joel's love story believable? Did it happen too quickly, or was it paced just right?

3. Ben's journal plays a major role in the story, from guiding him through the loss of his son to revisiting his love story with Abby. Do you believe in the power of letter writing? Have you ever kept a journal?

4. During the story, the readers see Abby and Ben's love story through flashbacks, and experience Abby and Joel falling in love in present time. Were you rooting for Abby to fall in love with Joel, or for her to hold out until Ben made it home?

5. What were your initial thoughts about Ben's secret, the letter he was reading when his plane went down, and the mysterious woman who kept showing up to Abby's house? Did your thoughts or hunches change while reading the novel?

6. How did you interpret Ben's time on the island, both while you were reading and after you finished the book? Did your interpretation change during your reading? Did Ben's journey surprise you?

7. How did you first interpret Joel's recurring dreams about looking for deer through the bay window of his childhood home, and the stranger appearing from the woods?

8. Abby's sister, Maggie, provides both guidance and comic relief during Abby's mourning. Do you have a "Maggie" in your life?

9. The holidays play an important role in the story, and Abby has a very different experience from the first holiday season she spends without Ben to the second. From the emotions they invoke, to the traditions that can run from one generation to the next, what are some of your favorite holiday rituals?

10. Did *Before I Go* make you laugh, cry, or both? Which parts of the novel were particularly moving or inspiring for you?

11. Let's talk about the ending. From Ben and Jacob to Rachel and Brian, from Joel and his father to the kid on the island, and each of these characters' connections to Abby—what was the biggest surprise for you?

12. Were you able to pick up on any of the clues throughout the story and guess any or all of the ending twists?

13. Is *Before I Go* a one-and-done novel, or do you see yourself reading it again? Have you ever read a book more than once?

14. Have you ever dreamt about a loved one after their passing? If so, did the dream provide closure, or did it serve some other purpose?

15. Do you believe we have guardian angels looking down on us?

Visit us online at
KensingtonBooks.com
to read more from your favorite authors,
see books by series, view reading
group guides, and more!

BOOK **CLUB**
BETWEEN THE **CHAPTERS**

Visit us online for sneak peeks, exclusive
giveaways, special discounts, author content,
and engaging discussions with your fellow readers.

Betweenthechapters.net

Sign up for our newsletters and be the first
to get exciting news and announcements about
your favorite authors!
Kensingtonbooks.com/newsletter